在路上

校尔康 著

周艺清 邵小燕 译

作家出版社

图书在版编目（CIP）数据

在路上 / 校尔康著. -- 北京：作家出版社，2022.11
ISBN 978-7-5212-1935-7

Ⅰ．①在… Ⅱ．①校… Ⅲ．①诗集 - 中国 - 当代
Ⅳ．①I227

中国版本图书馆CIP数据核字（2022）第109951号

在路上

作　　者：校尔康
出版统筹策划：汉　睿
装帧设计：孙惟静
责任编辑：翟婧婧
出版发行：作家出版社有限公司
社　　址：北京农展馆南里10号　　邮　　编：100125
电话传真：86-10-65067186（发行中心及邮购部）
　　　　　86-10-65004079（总编室）
E-mail:zuojia@zuojia.net.cn
http://www.zuojiachubanshe.com
印　　刷：北京盛通印刷股份有限公司
成品尺寸：130×185
字　　数：100千
印　　张：9.25
版　　次：2022年11月第1版
印　　次：2022年11月第1次印刷
ISBN　978-7-5212-1935-7
定　　价：58.00元

作者像

校尔康

姓校名卫，字尔康，号漫城过客，蒙古族（孛儿只斤氏）成吉思汗后裔，深信自然主义而自称城中隐者。曾在南京理工大学读书，后在南京珠江路谋生，并在南京九华山隐修三年，实证自我转变的疗愈力量后开始体验式写作并完成《活在当下的力量》。

已出版诗集《家：梦境中的流水》《在远方》《在路上》，著有佛教传奇首尊肉身比丘尼仁义法师传《九华山上的金刚之花》。诗集中部分作品《在远方》《一个人的河流》等被改编为同名民谣歌曲。

深信死亡是人生的一次旅行，无论是谁早晚都无法躲避；如果有所准备，无论何时我们都可无所畏惧。

让爱流动，有爱的地方就是天堂。

Xiao Erkang

Xiao Wei, style name Erkang, pseudonym Mancheng vacationer, who is a Mongolian, descendant of Genghis Khan, believes in naturalism and claimed to be a hermit in the city. Once studied in Nanjing University of Science and Technology, then he made a living in Zhujiang Road in Nanjing. Later he studied in Jiuhua Mountain in Nanjing for three years. After demonstrating the healing power of self-transformation, he began to write in an experiential way and complete a book named *Power of Living in the Present Moment*.

Published several collections of poetry, *Home*: *Running Water in Dreams*, *In the Distance and On the Road*. He also is the author of the biography of Master Renyi, which named *The Flower of Vajra on the Jiuhua Mountain*. Some of the works "In the Distancce" and "A Man's River" have been adapted into folk songs of the same name.

He believes that death is a journey of life, whether sooner or later nobody can escape. If prepared, whenever we can be fearless.

Let love flow, where there is love there is heaven.

周艺清（译者）

　　英文名 Joey，毕业于加拿大西蒙弗雷泽大学艺术与社会科学专业。喜欢中国传统文化，特别是茶文化。一直专注于现代文学的翻译工作，对现代诗有特殊的感情。

Zhou Yiqing

Joey was graduated from Simon Fraser University and majored in Arts and Social science. She likes traditional Chinese culture, especially tea culture. She always concentrates on translation of modern literature and has particular emotion to modern poems.

邵小燕（译者）

邵小燕，设计师，兼职翻译，长居南京。

Shao Xiaoyan

Shao Xiaoyan, designer, part-time translator, living in Nanjing.

目　录

破　执　　　*Moksanam*

爱是无量光 *Love is Amitqbha*

在行走中闭关　　*Being in silent retreat while walking*

序 言

Preface

在路上

文 / 校尔康

伯牙等不到子期，任高山流水，他把琴摔了。

梁武帝请达摩说禅，机缘未到法不轻传，他乘一苇渡江飘逸而去。

介子推死不言禄。晋文王报恩无门，却将他烧死在山中。怎么说？

有些人，有些事，为什么这样，只能慢慢悟。

你是谁？

我们常常忘记了自己。

那么，在我们静下来时和自己喝杯茶，静静地和自己说说话。

听一听，自己的声音。

我是谁？我将去哪里？

那个真实的自己在哪里？

在大江大河，还是深山野岭？在草原，还是海边？在乡村，还是城市？

喜欢粗茶淡饭，还是山珍海味？喜欢阳春白雪，还是禅茶一味？无一不好。

有的人想治理天下，有的人想游遍天下，有的人想富甲天下。

都没有错，平常心就是道。心安处即是禅悦，有和无都可以泰然清静地生活。

有的人在去南极的路上，有的人在攀登珠峰的路上，有的人在回家的路上。

成吉思汗手持上帝之鞭，横穿欧亚大陆，他的铁蹄征服了世界。但他没有征服自己。

二十世纪美国人杰克·凯鲁亚克在他的小说《在路上》说："因为我很贫穷，所以我拥有一切。"

现在的你，哪怕所有的都私人订制。

你拥有了一切，一切之一切。

又怎么样呢？

上下五千年，多少英雄豪杰，恰似一江春水向东流。世事变幻，如露亦如电。

在飞机上看云，云是这样。在山顶上看云，云是那样。云还是云，我还是我，法无高下，顺其自然。

上帝对人说：我医治你，是因为要伤害你。我爱你，是因为要惩罚你。

我们走路，骑车，乘船，坐车，坐飞机，乘游轮。从这个村到那个村，从这个城市到那个城市，从这个国家到那个国家，从这一站到那一站，说不清楚哪一站才是终点。

我们总以为没有经历过、没有拥有的是最好的。那些豪车洋房甚至飞机游艇总是代表成功。

经历过的人自然知道，就这样。

慢慢才明白，最奢侈的不是名车、名表，成为名人，原来最奢侈的是听自己的声音，和自己的灵魂在一起。

当你拥有了，经历了，你才发现生活还是这样没有改变，还是要吃饭，还是要睡觉。

慢慢才明白，无非是吃饭睡觉。

也就是和谁吃饭和谁睡觉。

这就是生活。

无论东方，还是西方。

所以要静心。

这就是生命的真相，无论你拥有多少，无论你经历多少。

你仍然是你。

在路上，需要不断地给予，需要静心的品质，需要爱的滋养。

父母是我们的天和地，是我们生命的源头。

那里包含着道。

老子一生默默无为而修，他得到了道。道法自然。

孔子仁爱天下获得了儒。

佛陀目睹明星，证悟成佛。

我来自哪里？

我们即使拥有飞机、游轮、珍宝又怎样？

我们即使走遍了全世界又怎样？

三界唯心。在通向自己的路上，将自己慢慢沉淀下来。世界上没有两片相同的雪花，也没有两片相同的叶子，这个世界上没有一样的自我。唯有自己，在独一无二的世界，可以去发现那种和自己相遇临在的寂静，那种宁静的虚无。

心无挂碍，活在当下。

大道至简，有爱的地方就是天堂。

On the Road

By Xiao Erkang

When Yu Boya, an adept in playing the dulcimer, lost his bosom friend Zhong Ziqi forever, he broke the dulcimer, no longer caring about the lofty mountains or the flowing water.

Emperor Wu of the Liang Dynasty asked Dharma to talk about Zen. But he failed to pick the right time, and Dharma left him, crossing the river by a piece of reed.

Jie Zitui refused to accept rewards when Prince Wen of Jin wanted to pay him for his help. The Prince set the mountain on fire to force Jie Zitui to show up, but the latter was burned alive unexpectedly. How should we understand such things?

For someone, something, why do they turn out like that? The answer comes to us only after some time as a result of enlightenment.

Who are you?

We often forget about ourselves.

Why not have a cup of tea and talk to yourself peacefully when you have time?

Listen to yourself.

Who am I? Where am I going?

Where is my true self?

Is he by massive rivers or on high mountain ridges? Is he in a grassland or by the seaside? Is he in a small village or in big cities?

Whether you like simple diets or epicurean delicacies, like highbrow art or simple Zen lessons, it's just fine, for there is nothing bad.

One wants to rule the populace; the other wants to tour around the world, and some others want to grow fabulous wealthy.

It's just fine. The way of nature lies in normal hearts. The joy of Zen lies in peace of mind. A calm life is possible no matter you have all or have none.

Some people are on their way to the Antarctica; some are on their way to the Mount Everest, and some are on their way home.

Genghis Khan, with God's whip in his hand, crossed Eurasia and conquered the world with his iron hooves. However, he never conquered himself.

Jack Kerouac, an American writer, said in his novel *On the Road* in the last century, "Everything belongs to me because I am poor."

Look at you, even if all your belongings are customized.

You hold all the cards, you have everything.

So what?

How many heroes have disappeared in the five thousand years of history, just like the spring river flowing east? The world changes, like a drop of dew dried in an instant, or like lightning, disappearing within a second.

You see different shapes of clouds, depending on whether you are in a plane or on the top of a mountain. No matter which shape you see, the cloud is still itself, so are you. For Dharma, none is the superior to any other, so let nature take its course.

God says to man, "I heal you therefore I hurt, love you therefore I punish."

We walk, cyde, take a boat or a car; take a plane or a cruise. We travel from this village to that village, from this city to that city, from this country to that country, from this station to that station. However, it is not clear which station is the destination.

We always think that those which we haven't experienced or haven't had the best. Luxury cars, houses and even airplanes and yachts are regarded as symbols of success. But once you have them, you will know that they are nothing special. Gradually we will realize that the most luxurious thing is to listen to your own voice and stay with your soul rather than the famous cars, luxury watches or becoming a celebrity.

You would find nothing has changed even if you owned or experienced much. You still need to eat and sleep. You will slowly understand that to eat and sleep are all you need. However, with whom do you eat and sleep?

That decides your life.

No matter whether you are in the East or the West, just ease your mind.

Whatever you own or experience, that is the truth of life.

You are still the original you.

When we are on the road, we need to provide

continuously, to have some meditation, to be nourished by love.

Parents are our heaven and earth, our origin of life.

There involves the way of nature.

Lao Zi, the founder of Taoism, spent his whole life to conform to nature which brought him to the truth of Taoism. The law of the Tao is to follow nature.

Confucius, the founder of Confucianism, with a heart of benevolence, gained Confucian thoughts.

The Buddha, seeing a flaming star, achieved his enlightenment.

Where are we from?

Even though we own airplanes, yachts or treasures,

so what?

Even if we tour around the world, so what?

In the three realms of Buddhism, all Dharmas are realized by mind. Let us slow down along the way towards ourselves. There are neither two identical snowflakes, nor two identical leaves in the world, and so are us. In our unique world, only you can meet the silent emptiness, where you shall find your soul.

Live in the moment, with no worries.

The greatest truths are the simplest. Where there is love, there is heaven.

诗为禅客添花锦，禅是诗家切玉刀

文／吴思敬

在诗歌界，校尔康身份很特殊。他爱诗习禅，出没于丛林，交友于十方，既是禅客，又是诗人。当读完校尔康的诗集《在路上》的时候，我想起了金代诗人元好问的两句诗"诗为禅客添花锦，禅是诗家切玉刀"。我觉得这两句诗不仅透辟地阐释了诗与禅的关系，同时也是理解校尔康其人其诗的一把钥匙。

冯友兰先生曾在《中国哲学简史》中指出："禅宗虽然是佛教的一个宗派，可是它对于中国哲学、文学、艺术的影响却是深远的。"禅是一种宗教，是一种哲学，同时也是一种隐秘的心灵体验。禅宗强调的是对时间的某种顿时的领悟，即所谓"永恒在瞬间"或"瞬间即为永恒"，其核心则是让生命超越现实的拘囿，从而进入永恒之中。禅宗希望超出人世烦恼，追求精神自由，但又不主张完全脱离世俗生活，不否定个体生命的幻想，适应了不同时代失意而苦闷的知识分子寻求精神解脱的愿望。禅看似不可言说，虚无缥缈，但真正走进去了，领悟了它，却能感受到它就在人们的日常生活当中，并与人的精神品格、思维方式、艺术素养等有密切的联系。

"自古诗情半个禅"，诗和禅一样，不提供定义，只是显示鲜活的情感与心灵状态。面对世界，禅家强调"身在万物中，心在万物上"，这与诗人主张的既要入乎其内又要出乎其外，颇有相通之处。细味那些传世的优秀诗歌，不仅能感受到音韵之美、意象之美，而且能领悟到蕴涵其中的哲理，能体味到溶解在生活中的秘密，而这与领悟禅机、禅趣，进入禅的境界，也确有某些异曲同工的地方。

禅宗认为，禅是不可言说的，要言说也要绕路而行，因而特别强调闻声悟道、见色明心，强调暗示性，所谓"佛祖拈花，迦叶微笑"是也。冯友兰说："禅宗中人常说：善说者终日道如不道，善闻者终日闻如不闻。宗杲说：'上士闻道，如印印空。中士闻道，如印印水。下士闻道，如印印泥。'（《大慧普觉禅师语录》卷二十）印印空无迹，如所谓'羚羊挂角，无迹可寻'。"而这又恰与诗人审美创造中的思维方式得以沟通。诗人在创作中同样强调一种"悟性"，所谓"鸟啼花落，皆与神通。人不能悟，付之飘风。唯我诗人，众妙扶智，但见性情，不著文字"（袁枚：

《续诗品·神悟》）。优秀的诗作都具有这种暗示性，强调含不尽之意于言外，强调表达的疏密得当、不即不离，具有一种含蓄、空灵之美。由禅悟到诗歌创作的直觉思维，由禅境到追求无言之美的诗境，一脉相承，成了中国诗学中非常重要的传统。

陆游晚年给他的儿子陆子遹写过一首诗，提出"汝果欲学诗，工夫在诗外"（《示子遹》）。意思是说，一个诗人写诗，光在文字、技巧上下功夫是不够的，更重要的是要在阅历、才智、学养、操守、精神品格等方面下功夫。这一点，对禅诗的写作者来说尤其重要。

应当说，作为一个诗人，校尔康是很重视诗外功夫的。他曾在九华山带发修行，追随传灯法师学禅修道。他对佛学禅思早已不是停留在知识层面上的了解，而是个真正的悟道者了。我也读过校尔康的散文，在《悲伤的终点是爱》这篇散文中，诗人描绘了自己悟道的感受：

当我在玄武湖边上行走，落日的余晖投射在静静的湖上，对面的紫金山静如处子，在博大的寂静中，我融入这样的风景。

我觉得我已不在！

我经常会碰到一些人，他们经历过生死的磨砺而充满爱。一位刘姓师兄带领一个上百人的学佛小组，其中有十来位身患癌症八十多岁的老人。他们在一起去很远的地方朝山，融入到团队中，有活动时大家自带干粮和水，我经常碰到他们，在相处的短暂时光里我会被他们的淡然平和、超越恐惧的光芒照耀。人的心灵所需的物品，是用钱买不到的。我采访过其中的几个人，他们都乐观地说："我们想阿弥陀佛会来接我们的。"这种超凡忘我的境界给了我深深的记忆。

校尔康以禅客之心，在禅界和尘世间往复融通，在悟到生死之间的无常后开始追求快乐的人生与解脱的境界，在红尘滚滚的世界里重新找回自己，在信仰世界的神秘空间中获得了无尽的创造力。他的诗歌有禅诗之灵思，兼偈语之警策，述说着世人的感情和觉悟，成为佛光照耀下的当代生活之回响。

校尔康曾在自己的诗作中描写了在礼佛过程中悟道瞬间的独特感受："那一天 / 登上莲台 / 供上万盏禅灯 / 心念无限的祝愿 / 漫山吉祥的佛号 / 温暖不了我的泪水 // 我受持无上的真言 / 融化在光明中 / 多少甘露 / 从天而降 / 可是我 / 浑然不知 // 那一天 / 遇到你 / 春暖花开 / 才知因缘熟了。"（《那一天》）随着这种"悟"而来的，是那种心无挂碍的人生态度，如他所言：

在通向自己的路上，将自己慢慢沉淀下来。世界上没有两片相同的雪花，也没有两片相同的叶子，这个世界上没有一样的自我。唯有自己，在独一无二的世界，可以去发现那种和自己相遇临在的寂静，那种宁静的虚无。

心无挂碍，活在当下。

大道至简，有爱的地方就是天堂。

正是这种"心无挂碍"的人生态度，使他的诗歌呈现了诗思与禅境相交融的灵性书写的高度，从而与当下诗歌中的大量平庸之作划清了界线。

在《留得残荷听雨声》中，面对九月湖边的残荷，沐浴着蒙蒙细雨，诗人默然心动，悟出的是"花开花谢佛自在 / 山上山下真如意"的空前自由的天地。

在《在河边》中，面对夕阳西下、暮色花影，诗人静静地体会时空的安宁，体验着"空"，发出"这个世界上还有什么能与寂静同在 / 寂静之美胜于无声的世界"的感慨。

在《自由》中，面对窗外黄昏中，一只在飞翔、将纤细的身影横穿天空的鸟，他在鸟儿留下的"白色的弧"中，悟出了生命的奥义：自由被扭曲在规范之中，一切虚妄的幸福都宛如昙花。

在《与光同尘》中，诗人发现阳光普照的光线中，隐藏着"无数的灰尘／一边发光／一边飞扬"，从而悟出"人生的光线／不也是时亮时灭／闪闪烁烁"，进而渴望"无量的光明／穿越山川河流／让整个寂静的人生／和大地同生／与光同尘"。

上引的几首诗，是校尔康有代表性的作品，均属于禅诗。诗人受身边自然景象的触发，灵光一闪，怦然心动，诗情与禅意相交汇，一首首诗歌就这样诞生了。

禅诗的写作，在中国有悠久的传统。在我看来，禅诗的写作大致可分为三个层次。第一个层次是字面上并无佛理禅思的痕迹，呈现在读者面前的是由优美的意象构成的画面，佛理禅思寓于其中，可让人思而悟之，味而得之。王维的《鸟鸣涧》《辛夷坞》《鹿柴》《山居秋暝》等可视为这类作品的代表。第二个层次是诗人以精心选择的意象，构成一个生动的画面和场景，并用文字把诗人所悟出的佛理禅思点出来。第三个层次则不借助意象或画面，直接把诗人悟出的佛理禅思说出来。

如果对照这三个层次，应当说校尔康对第一层次的诗是心向往之，但目前还不能说已写出与前人成功之作相匹配的作品。他的比较优秀的诗作，基本属于第二层次，有来自生活的意象与画面，多以卒章显志的方式，保留着对佛理禅思的言说。此外，校尔康还有一些属于第三层次的作品，诸如《爱是一种承诺》《我们的人生需要旅行》等篇章，诗人隐去了与自然意象相关的内容，直接把他悟出的佛理禅思向读者倾吐出来。这部分诗歌通常以禅理的雄辩与机锋的敏锐征服读者，从张扬佛理禅思以及健康的人生哲学而言，自有一定的价值，但没有了优美的意象，也就失去了诗味的绵长，距离真正的禅诗毕竟隔了一层。当然，以校尔康的悟性，他会不断调整自己的写作策略与方向，其诗思诗艺精进的空间是可以想象的。

2015年校尔康出版了他的第一部诗集《在远方》，现在他的第二部诗集《在路上》又将出版。我因思忖，在当下的时代，怀着一种崇高的宗教情怀，希望用爱来化解喜怒情仇，渴求用佛理禅思普度众生，这样的诗人实在是太难得了。因此不揣浅陋，特撰此文予以评述并推荐，是为序。

Poetry Adds Splendor to a Zen Stylite, While Zen Provides a Poet with a Jade-Cutting Knife.

By Wu Sijin

In the field of poetry, Xiao Erkang has a very special identity. He loves both poetry and Zen. He hides away from the maddening crowds while making friends in a wide range. He is not only a Zen stylite, but also a poet. When I finished reading Xiao's collection of poems *On the Road*, it reminds me of two lines written by Yuan Haowen, a poet of the Jin Dynasty, "Poetry adds splendor to a Zen stylite, while Zen provides a poet with a jade-cutting knife". I think these two lines not only explicate the relationship between poetry and Zen, but also work as a key to understand Xiao and his poems.

In the book *A Short History of Chinese Philosophy*, Feng Youlan once pointed out that "Although Zen is a sect of Buddhism, it has a far-reaching influence on Chinese philosophy, literature and art." Zen is a religion, a philosophy while it is also a secret spiritual experience. Zen emphasizes a kind of instant understanding of time, which is, the so-called "eternity in an instant" or "an instant represents the eternal". Its core is to make your life transcend the constraints of reality and enter the eternity. Zen suggests going beyond the troubles of the world and pursuing spiritual freedom. But it does not mean completely breaking away from the secular life or denying the fantasy of individual life. In fact, it adapts to the aspirations of frustrated and depressed Chinese intellectuals in different times to seek spiritual liberation. Zen seems to be unspeakable and illusory. However, when you really comprehend it, you can feel it is in people's daily life and closely related to people's spiritual character, thinking mode, artistic quality, etc.

"Zen is implicated by poetry all the time". Poetry, which is the same as Zen, does not provide a definition, but only shows fresh emotions and a spiritual state. When facing the world, Zen emphasizes "the body among everything, and the heart beyond everything", which has something in common with Xiao's idea that we should not only keep close relationship with the secular but also know how to retreat from it. If you savor the excellent poems handed down, you will not only feel the beauty of sounds and images, but also the philosophy and secret of life contained in them. This is also similar to the process of understanding the Buddhist allegorical words and gestures and to the realm of Zen.

The Zen sect believes that Zen is unspeakable, and even if we want to speak it, we should do it in a circuitous way. Therefore, it emphasizes paying special attention to recognize the truth among vocal and visional signals, as is suggested in the saying "Tathagata picks up a flower and Kasyapa smiles". Feng Youlan said: "People in the Zen sect often say that it is better for people good at speaking not to speak, people good at listening not to listen. The Zen master Zonggao once said, 'The wisest people listen to the senses, as if it is empty. The wiser people listen to the senses, as if it is water. The general people listen to the senses, as if it is mud.' (Volume 20 of *Zen Master Dahui Pujue's Quotes*) Emptiness is the truth, which is just like "an antelope sleeping by hanging its horns on the tree, so no trace can be found after it is gone."

Such Zen belief, however, happens to connect with the thinking mode of a poet during his aesthetic creation. A poet also emphasizes a kind of "savvy" in his creation, as expressed in such lines as "a singing bird and a falling flower, are both connected to Zen. If you cannot understand that, they will be lost in the wind. Only a poet, who assimilates all kinds of beauty to build his wisdom, conveys his feelings beyond words." (Yuan Mei:

"Continuation of Poetry Savoring—Divine Understanding")

Excellent poems all manage to be implicit, emphasizing the meaning beyond words and the appropriateness and justness of expression, which produces a containing spiritual beauty. The idea of "intuition", developed from Zen study to poetry writing as well as the idea of "realm", introduced from Zen into poetry focusing on the beauty beyond words, thus have become very important traditions in Chinese poetry.

In his later years, Lu you wrote a poem to his son Lu Ziyu, saying, "if you want to be a poet, the effort you make should be beyond poetry." ("A Lesson to Ziyu") He means that when a poet writes poems, it is not enough to work on words and skills alone. The more important things are hard-working on accumulating experience, intelligence, knowledge, merits and spiritual quality, etc. This is especially important for a writer who writes Zen poems.

It should be said that, as a poet, Xiao works hard at non-poetry fields. He once practiced Buddhism in Jiuhua

Mountain and followed Master Chuanzhen to learn Zen. His understanding of Dharma is no longer limited to the verbal level, and reaches the level of enlightenment. I have also read Xiao's prose. In the prose "Love is the End of Sorrow", the poet describes his experience about an enlightenment.

When I walk by the Xuanwu Lake, the afterglow of the setting sun is projected on the quiet lake. The opposite Zijin Mountain stands as quiet as a virgin. In the vast silence, I am integrated into the landscape.

I think I am no longer a single self!

I often meet people who are full of love after the experience of death. A senior Buddhist follower Mr. Liu is the leader of a group of more than 100 Buddhists, including more than ten elderly people in their eighties who have cancer. They often make a pilgrimage to a faraway temple on mountain. Everyone brings his own food and water.

In the short time when I get along with them, I am always illuminated by their calmness and peace beyond fear. What people need for their soul cannot be bought with money. I interviewed several people among them. They all said optimistically that they believe Amitabha would guide their way. This extraordinary state of selflessness deeply impressed me.

Xiao Erkang, who shuttles between the world of Zen and the mortal world with all his heart, also begins to pursue a happy life and a state of liberation after realizing the capriciousness of life and death. He regains himself in the world of mortals and harvests endless creativity in the mysterious space of belief. His poems are full of inspiration from Zen and lessons of Buddhist maxims, which narrates worldly feelings and the consciousness of the existing world, thus becoming an echo of the contemporary life in the light of Buddhism.

In his poems, Xiao Erkang once described the unique

feeling of epiphany during a Buddhist worship: "On that day / I ascended the lotus seat / Enshrining thousands of Zen lamps / praying for endless wishes / With auspicious Buddha horn over hill and dale / My tears failed to be warmed / I observed the supreme mantra / Melting in the light / So much dew / fell from the sky / But I / Didn't notice them / On that day / When I met you /Spring suddenly blossomed /And I knew finally that time had ripened our life." ("On That Day"). With this kind of "awakenings" comes the kind of unhindered attitude towards life. As he said: "Let us slow down along the way towards ourselves. There are neither two identical snowflakes, nor two identical leaves in the world, and so are us. In our unique world, only you can meet the silent emptiness, where you shall find your soul.

Live in the moment, with no worries.

The greatest truths are the simplest. Where there is love, there is heaven".

It is this kind of "unhindered" attitude towards life that brings his poems to the height of spiritual writing which blends poetic inspirations and Zen, thus drawing a clear line between itself and the large numbers of mediocre works in contemporary poetry.

In "The Sound of Rain with Withered Lotus", looking at the dying lotus in the lake of September, bathed in the drizzle, the poet was touched silently, and realized an unprecedented sense of freedom in which "Things come and go/The mountain sits still".

In "By the River", facing the sunset and flowers in the dusk, the poet quietly enjoyed the peace of time and space, experiencing "emptiness", and lamented "What else in the world can be compared with silence? / The beauty of silence goes beyond the silent world itself".

In "Freedom", looking at a bird, flying in the dusk

outside the window, he realized the meaning of life in the "white arc" left by the bird: freedom is distorted by norms and all fake happiness is just like the short-lived epiphyllum.

In "To Cover the Glare, and to Mix with the Dust", the poet found that "There are countless dust/Glowing/While flying" in the sunlight. He realized that "The light of life, too/Flickers at random/Twinkles from time to time". He yearns for "Boundless light/Shines over mountains and rivers/Making the whole silent life/Grow with the earth/With the light, and with the dusts".

The poems quoted above are the representative works of Xiao Erkang, all of which are Zen poems. Triggered by the natural scene around him, the poet is full of inspiration and enthusiasm, and a poem appears when poetic thoughts meet Zen.

The writing of Zen poems has a long tradition in

China. In my opinion, Zen poem writing can be roughly divided into three levels. The first level includes poems without literal traces of Buddhism or Zen thoughts. What is presented in front of the readers are idyllic pictures, in which are contained Buddhist or Zen thoughts to inspire readers. Wang Wei's "Bird-singing stream", "Magnolia Retreat", "The Deer Enclosure" and "Autumn Evening in the Mountains" can be regarded as the representatives of such works. In the second level, poets carefully select images form a vivid picture, and point out the Buddhist or Zen thoughts related with words. The third level, without images or pictures, poets directly write down the Buddhist or Zen thoughts.

Concerning these three levels, we should say that Xiao Erkang is eager for the first, but we still can't say that he has written poems that can be compared with those masterpieces in history. His best poems basically belong to the second level, which introduce Buddhism and Zen thoughts in words, images and pictures from life.

In addition, he has some poems belonging to the third level, such as "Love is a Promise" and "Our Life Needs to Travel", in which he omits natural images and directly pours out his Buddhist and Zen thoughts to readers. This part of poetry usually conquers readers with eloquence in Buddhist thoughts and the sharpness of wit. From the aspect of propagating Buddhist or Zen thoughts and a healthy philosophy of life, such poems have certain value. However, without beautiful images, they lack poetic flavor. After all, they have some distance with real Zen poetry. Of course, Xiao Erkang, with his savvy, will constantly adjust his writing strategy and direction. It is convincible he will make great progress in his poems in the future.

In 2015, Xiao Erkang published his first collection of poems *In the Distance*, and now his second collection of poems *On the Road* is coming out. I believe nowadays it is precious that a poet, with lofty religious feelings, would still desire to use love to resolve the problems of anger and hatred and to free all livings from torments with Buddhist or Zen thought. Therefore, with gratitude, I write this article for comment and recommendation of Xiao's collection of poems.

执 着

Upadana

在路上

在路上

我不辞辛苦

转山转水

只想遇到你

在路上

我顶礼焚香

一心一意

就想求到你

在路上

我戒情戒义

时时刻刻

皈依你

在路上

我从从容容

无知无觉

就路过了你

在路上

我和你同行

却发现

终点不一

在路上

我们只观此生

悟到了如来

却到不了彼岸

On the Road

On the road

Take all the trouble

I walk around mountains and lakes

Hoping to encounter you.

On the road

I worship and burn incense

With heart and soul

Eager to pray for you.

On the Road

I cut off my love and emotions

At every moment

Always trying to convert to you.

On the road

I take my time

Without noticing

I pass by you.

On the road

I am with you

But suddenly I found

Different endings for us.

On the road

We only see this life

Enlightened of the Buddha

While reaching no Faramita.

我

我的头发长满树枝

在心灵上蔓延

在出售鲜花的年代

我忽然觉得

自己正努力变成

花的姿态

I

Branches are mingled in my hair

Spread in my heart.

In the flower-selling era,

I suddenly feel

I am turning into

A flower's shape.

你看不到

你看不到

心在哪里

虚空

就在哪里

你看不到

心

微笑

又恍如虚空

你看不到

心

应如所住

又何住

深如大海

尽管

泪涌如泉

尽管

又静如虚空

你看不到

心

如梦幻泡影

又细至针尖

你看不到

但心

亦非是虚空

又是虚空

于是

喜悦

于是

无住

You Never See

You never see

Where love is,

Where void is.

You never see

The heart

Smiling

Is just like void.

You never see

The heart

Should dwell somewhere.

But how?

As deep as the sea.

Although

Tears run like a flood

Although

Silence is like void.

You never see

The heart

Is like a fantastic illusion

Or is thin as a needle tip.

You never see

The heart

Is not void

While void still.

Then

Be joyful,

Then

Stay free.

观心：境之乱

站在一种高处

才会有

一身的寒意

在你灵魂的深处

乱如麻丝

智者的预知

得到盲者的回应

这是一种不幸

心灵的沙漠

开满花朵

误为花开飘香

笑为顿悟

伟大的东西恰恰不幸

创造是天才的行为

静坐　观心

我将如何独自去散步

将虚妄去除

因为一种思想的快乐

体现一种遐想的风度

Reading the Heart: The Chaos

Standing at some height, where

A chill swallows you up.

Deeply in your soul

Is all mess.

Predictions of the wise,

Win only a response from the blind

How unfortunate it is.

Desert of the heart,

Is full of flowers

Mistaken for fragrance of blooms,

Laughter is like epiphany,

Misfortune is just a great thing.

Creating is a genius act

Sitting still, observing the mind

How would I walk alone?

Wipe off the illusions

With the mind's happiness

Show a demeanor of reveries.

上帝还是佛

上帝　还是佛

我是人

神爱世人

佛度众生

我是人

我是一个人

看着死亡

看着缓慢地老去

我的心

已容得下沧海

God or Buddha

God or Buddha, I am a man.

For God so loving the world,

For Buddha delivering all beings.

I am a man, a human being.

When watching death, watching the slow withering,

My heart,

Can bear the vast.

圣诞快乐：问问那棵树吧

一个人坐在屋子里

对面是一棵树

想起一个朋友

不知他过得怎样

不想打电话

也不想写信

那就问问那棵树吧

它点点头

然后

它又摇摇头

想起去过的一个地方

不知有没有变样

不想打电话了解

也不想上网查询

那就问问那棵树吧

它点点头

又摇摇头

想起一个诗意的黄昏

那一刻有些莫名地惆怅

也不知道未来的哪一天

它还会不会出现

那就问问那棵树吧

它点点头

又摇摇头

有的人从生命中走了

就再也没有回来

有的人在你身边

却常常让你熟视无睹

究竟为什么

那就问问那棵树吧

它点点头

后又摇摇头

Merry Christmas: Ask that tree

Sitting alone in the room,

Opposite is a tree.

I thought of a friend,

Wondering how he was.

I wouldn't make phone calls,

Nor would I write any letters.

Ask that tree then.

It nodded,

And

Shook its head.

I thought of a place I've been,

Wondering how it was.

I wouldn't make any phone calls,

Nor would I check it online.

Then ask that tree.

It nodded,

And

Shook its head.

Thinking of a poetic dusk,

An odd empty feeling crept upon my heart.

I wondered what day in the future,

It would appear again.

Then ask that tree.

It nodded

And

Shook its head.

Some people walk away from your life,

And never come back

Some are around you

But often you turn a blind eye to them.

Why?

Ask that tree

It nodded

Then shook its head.

大吉祥云：烟花散时虚空无尽

过年了

处处祥云

众云

大光明云

大吉祥云

大慈悲云

当下升起的情绪是寂静的

炸裂过后烟花散尽

突然发现进入了一个虚空

在所有因缘和合的时候

那是一个中心

世界的中心

虚空有尽

我愿无穷

面对尘世的世俗

什么才是最好的

没有理由

这些年都这么过了

当然还是要顺其自然地过下去

时间不可以重复

过去了就过去了

来了也就来了

Auspicious Clouds:
Endless Void after the Fireworks

In a Chinese New Year, auspicious clouds are everywhere.

Multiple clouds are there,

Great bright clouds,

Great auspicious clouds,

And great compassionate clouds.

The emotions aroused at that moment are silent.

After the explosion, the fireworks were scattered.

I suddenly found myself in a void.

The time of all karma being harmonious,

That is a core,

A center of the world.

The emptiness has an end

I'd rather be infinite.

Facing the secular world,

What is the best?

There is no reason.

All these years have gone by,

Nature will surely take its course.

Time cannot be repeated,

The past is past,

When it comes, it comes.

问禅：花之心

大寒时节

禅者带着侍者来用茶

在落花的茶树下停下脚步

侍者说

师父

花落了

真好看

师问

花有心吗

答

有的

师问

花的心

在哪里

答

当然

花蕊中

师问

你看到了吗

答

是的

在里面

禅者拿起那枝花

花瓣随风落下

他举着空枝

问

花心在哪里

侍者默然无语

停了片刻

问

师父

花有心吗

禅者说

有

我在一旁

听得欢喜

赶紧合十礼拜二人

Ask Zen: Heart of Flowers

On the day of Great Cold,

The master took the attendant to have tea.

They stopped under the flower-falling tea tree.

The attendant said,

Master,

Flowers are falling,

How beautiful they are.

The master asked,

Does the flower have a heart?

The answer came,

Yes.

The master asked,

Where is the heart of a flower?

The answer came,

Of course, it is in the stamen.

The master asked,

Do you see that?

The answer came,

Yes.

It's inside.

The master picked up a flower,

Whose petals fell in the wind

He held up the empty branch,

Asked,

Where is the flower heart?

The attendant was silent.

After a while

He asked,

Master,

Does the flower have a heart?

The master answered,

Yes.

I, on their side, listened with a bliss,

Put my palms together to pay homage to them.

留得残荷听雨声

路过

路过

想起九月的荷花

今天湖边的清风不在

空蒙雨雾

东边这角的荷花早就谢了

这一年又要过去了

这一年又来了

求问一位成道者的踪迹

幸遇良知引见一位道人

说明缘由

道人号"山里人"

来偈

无人迹处有奇观

世事崎岖履薄冰

我想了想这几天的花景

复

花开花谢佛自在

山上山下真如意

可能

相差太远

心不能印

僧者打坐了

于是我也坐了一会儿

走了出来

看看湖边的残荷

对着蒙蒙的细雨

不禁想起这句话

默然

The Sound of Rain with Withered Lotus

Passing by

Passing by

I thought of the September lotus,

While gone is the lake breeze

Now there was only a drizzle and haze

Lotus in the east corner has withered.

The year is drawing to a close.

The year is coming again.

I wanted to trace some enlightened saint,

And was luckily introduced to a Taoist.

I explained the reason,

The Taoist, named Hillbilly Man,

Answered in a verse:

Miracles appear in deserted places,

To live in the world is like treading on the ice.

Thinking of the flowers

I answered,

Things come and go

The mountain sits still

Perhaps,

The distance between us was too big

To reach a mutual affinity

The monk sat in meditation,

And I sat for a while, too.

I walked out

Looking at the remnant lotus by the lake

Facing the drizzle

I couldn't help remembering this sentence

And I could do nothing but be silent.

花之语

顿时花开

处处飘香

最是

人间四月天

花之期

自然行道

花无心

但香溢四野

春暖花开

是豁达的心境

坦然地接受

是自然的臣服

原来人世间

幸福之道

无一法可得

唯一心可造

Flower Language

Flowers bloomed in a sudden and

Everywhere is fragrant.

The most wonderful time is

An April day.

The season of flowering,

Follows the law of nature.

The flowers, unintentionally,

Send fragrance around.

A full spring,

Is like an open mind.

The calm acceptation

Is the submission to nature.

The way of happiness

In this human world

Cannot be found by laws,

And can only be reached with your heart.

雨后落花：带我穿过山门

一、空

冬天怎么会有花

门前的茶花

一边在开一边在落

落花的枝头就这样空了

枝头上还挂着绿叶

绚丽的落花

华丽洒脱地盖在草地上

昨天正好下着雨

早晨雨停了

可是还有风

风一吹

枝头一摇

这是世上最自由的树

我理了理枝头茂密的地方

花瓣就不经意地掉下来

我忽然觉得

多事的人啊

风有点冷

毕竟是冬天

落花的世界

美得惊心

二、无相

河边一群鸟

飞起

我走到屋里拿了一碗米

撒下

然后

我等着鸟什么时候能来

我轻轻地问自己

何时我能懂鸟语

都说万物皆有灵性

生公说法顽石点头

这鸟至少比我更有觉性

它怎么就能知道我会来喂它

可鸟们

一句话未说

我却说了许多话

我抓了一把落花抛到水里

风一吹有些飘进水里

有的落到脚边

三、解脱

一只鸟

破空而鸣

落花流水

生命无常

在一念间

照见五蕴皆空

这心头的世界突然发现有无限的寂静

让我想到那句

不生不灭

不垢不净

不增不减

人世间的沧桑与世间人的悲伤突然升起

花开花落

来去自如

面对这场花宴

本来就想深情地大哭一场

花儿都这么自在

这世界怎么会这么地让人彻底清凉

干脆就放开大哭

泪奔如流

真是痛快

Falling Flowers after the Rain: Take me through the Monastery Gate

1. Emptiness

How can there be flowers in winter?

The camellia in front of the door

Is blooming while falling.

The branches, when flowers are gone, are left empty

While green leaves are still hanging from them.

Gorgeous falling flowers

Luxuriantly and freely cover the grass.

It happened to rain yesterday

In the morning stopped the rain

But there is still wind.

The wind blows

The branches shake.

This is the freest tree in the world.

I took care of the thick branches

While petals falling off inadvertently.

Suddenly I felt

I was really meddling for nothing.

The wind is a bit cold

This is winter, after all.

The world of the fallen petals

Is stunningly beautiful.

2. No Formlessness

Birds by the river

Were flying up.

I went to the house and got a bowl of rice

I sprinkled the rice,

And,

Waited for the birds to come.

I asked myself gently

When could I understand the birds, twitter?

It's believed that all things have a soul

A word from the wise is sufficient.

The birds seemed to be more intelligent than me

Or how did they know I was going to feed them?

But the birds

Said nothing.

While I said a lot.

I grabbed some fallen flowers and threw them to the

water.

Some were blown into the water

Some fell to my feet.

3. Mokṣa

A bird,

Sings through the silent air.

Flowers fall and water flows,

Life is such a capricious one.

In a breath,

Light shedding on the five skandhas and finding them equally empty.

The world in my heart is found to be infinitely silent suddenly.

It reminds me of such a line: Neither produced nor destroyed;

Neither defiled nor immaculate;

Neither increasing nor decreasing.

The vicissitudes and sadness of the world come to

my heart suddenly.

Flowers bloom and flowers fade,

All things just go naturally.

Facing such a feast of flowers,

I want to cry bitterly.

Flowers are growing so naturally

How could the world be so cool?

Just let go and cry

Pour out the tears,

And what a delight!

与光同尘

这一天

对着玻璃

透过被折射的阳光

觉察到透明的细节

我发现光线里隐藏

无数的灰尘

一边发光

一边飞扬

想想这个世界

一沙一粒

一尘一蒂

有多少真假

多少的明暗同时存在

一切尽在眼前

人生的光线

不也是时亮时灭

闪闪烁烁

都在说四大皆空

成住坏空

一切幻化

风大

火大

水大

地大

人这一辈子

了知全部的真相

也终究变成了

无量的光芒

也是无数的灰尘

一转眼

多少的时光

五味杂陈

从生到死

我们亲自送走

多少的人

或男或女

或老或少

他们在四大皆空中

幻化成灰尘

飘散风中

多少因缘聚合

又降临多少新的生命

人这一生

两手空空

从无到有

又从有到无

来时流泪水分充足

走时含笑火性十足

不管有过什么

都要统统地交还大地

一笑间

大是大非

生生灭灭

一切本来是空

天天吃饭

天天睡觉

可是谁又了知

这空

如同光影同尘

只要让心轻松下来

这个空

犹如在无限的虚空

空空的心

无边无际

无量的寂静

和万物大同

哪怕是一世的虚荣

一身的奇迹

一生的光荣

也无法永生

这个空

让心抵达虚无

这个空

让心了苦

无量的光明

穿越山川河流

让整个寂静的人生

和大地同生

与光同尘

To Cover the Glare, and to Mix with the Dust

One day

I stand in front of a piece of glass

Through the refracted sunlight

I perceive the transparent details.

Hidden in the light

There are countless dust

glowing

While flying.

Thinking of the world,

A sand, a grain

A dust, a stem.

The true and the false,

The light and the dark, they all coexist.

Everything is in front of us.

The light of life, too

Flickers at random,

Twinkles from time to time.

Emptiness is all.

The four elements are nothing but fantasies.

Wind, fire, water and earth.

In this life, you

Knowing all the truth

Still you are going to be some

Boundless light

Or uncountable dust

In a twinkling

Time flying, emotions mixing.

From birth to death,

We wave goodbye to

So many people.

Man or woman; old or young.

They go into the void,

Changing into dust, gone in the wind.

How many Karmas are harmonized?

How many new lives are born?

All your life,

You come with empty hands,

Growing from nothing to something,

Then leaving from something to nothing.

You come with tears, full of water.

You go with smiles, full of fire.

Whatever you have had,

Will be given back to the earth.

With a smile,

You experience right and wrong,

Life and death,

Emptiness is all.

You eat every day,

You sleep every day,

But who really knows that.

This emptiness,

Is everywhere just like light, like dust.

Just relax your heart.

This emptiness,

Is like an infinite void.

An empty heart,

is limitless.

The boundless silence

Is united with everything.

Even a lifetime's fame,

All the miracles

And the lifelong glory,

Cannot exist forever.

This emptiness

Sends your heart to the nihility.

This emptiness,

Stops your heart from feeling bitterness.

Boundless light,

Shines over mountains and rivers,

Making the whole silent life,

Grow with the earth,

With the light, and with the dusts.

破　执

Moksanam

心生便是罪生时

真空是

人们与心灵间

纯洁的连接

如果

为了一点利益

去改变

空就会

轻易地切断

自由的心灵

就会

蒙上灰尘

转变了

心

念

就改变了

你的

全世界

Sin Occurs When Feelings Occur

The emptiness is

What is between people and their soul

It's a pure connection.

If

For a little benefit

You change that,

The emptiness will

Be easily broken

The free mind

Will

Be dim with dust.

Changing

The mind

Will change

Your

Whole world.

抱残守缺：今天就是不完美

太好了

今天就是不完美

没有什么遗憾

就抱着那个遗憾待一会儿

水月镜花

水还是水

花还是花

遗憾是水中的月

镜中的花

看得见的是相

看不见的是缘

抱残守缺

大拙大美

人生最大的挑战就是完美

何必和自己过不去

去假存真

随缘

就是爱

To Stick to the Broken and the Imperfect: Today is not Perfect

Fine

Today is not perfect

No regret for that

For a while, just live with such regrets.

The moon is in the water and flowers are in the

mirror,

Water is water,

Flowers are flowers.

Why regret for the moon in the water,

or for the flowers in the mirror?

What you can see is the form,

What you can't see is the fate.

Stick to the broken and the imperfect

Extremely imperfect is extremely beautiful.

To reach perfection is the greatest challenge in our life.

Why go against yourself ?

Getting rid of the false, keep to the truth,

and go naturally, that is what love means.

门：在路上

当你来到这个世界

你以为你是谁

其实

你

谁

也

不

是

当你成为你自己

你将不再是你

经云：

一切有为法

如梦幻泡影

如露亦如电

应作如是观

心

安在路上

觉醒

才会

自然而然地发生

The Door: On the Road

When you come to this world,

Who do you think you are?

In fact,

You

are

Nothing.

When you become yourself,

You will no longer be yourself.

Buddhist sutras say that,

All conditioned phenomena are like a dream, an

illusion,

A bubble and a shadow,

Like dew and lightning.

Thus, please look at the world in this way.

A heart

Peacefully on the road

Awakening

Will

Naturally happen.

门与道

重重之门

都是道

但常常

是无路可走

处处

似十字路口

本来

什么门

都没有

本来

什么路

都可走

从未体验过

就不会

自然生长

Doors and Ways

Doors over doors,

Are the ways,

But often

There is no way

Everywhere

Is like a crossroads.

At first,

There are,

No doors at all,

At first,

Any ways

Can be picked.

Never experiencing

One would never

Naturally grow.

慢慢地静下来

慢慢地静下来

点上一支香

用所有身心

熏习清凉

慢慢地静下来

点上一盏灯

用所有的光

照亮灰暗

慢慢地静下来

倒一杯水

让所有的心思

柔软清凉

慢慢地静下来

弯腰

俯身

礼拜

慢慢地合十

忏悔

冥想

心

安放与飘荡

To Slow Down

Slow down,

Get an incense.

With all your heart,

Receive the purity and coolness.

Slow down,

Light a lamp,

With its ray,

Light up the gloom.

Slow down,

Get a glass of water,

Let the mind,

Be soft and pure.

Slow down,

Stoop

Bend over

Worship

Slowly get palms together.

Confess,

Meditate

Your heart

Will be calm and free.

即使，于是

即使你给了我

千匹宝马

我也无法

远走天涯

即使

远隔千山万水

我怎么还觉得

你近在心湖

即使你给了我

完美的天堂

我却无法搭上

上天的云梯

即使

在那清净的刹土

也摄不住

想你的心神

即使

你给了我

一座城池

我也做不了

那一方的诸侯

即使

你一笑倾城

也只能

拈花而过

即使

你给了我

一生的繁华

我也不能做

你的烟花

于是

你给了我

万顷福田

无上的真言

依然无花又无果

Even, Then

Even if you give me

Thousands of horses,

Still I can't

Walk away.

Then

Even if

We are far away from each other,

I still feel

You are by my side.

Even if you give me

A perfect heaven,

Still I can't climb

The ladder of cloud.

Then

Even

The pure land

Cannot hold

my mind.

Even if

You give me

A city,

Still I can't

Be lord of that land.

Then

Even if

You have a fascinating smile,

I can only

Gently pass you.

Even if

You give me

a lifelong wealth,

Still I can't

Be your fireworks.

Even if

You give me

Boundless blessed land,

And supreme mantra,

There still will be no flower or fruit.

不管

不管你信或不信

你都是一盏灯

有时亮

有时暗

不管你懂或不懂

你都是一本书

有时读读

有时放放

不管你理或不理

你都是一座山

有时想翻

有时想看

不管你知或不知

你都是道

走也过

不走也过

于是我和你

不远不近

于是我和你

不坐不静

No matter

Whether you believe or not,

You are always a light.

Sometimes bright

Sometimes dark.

Whether you understand or not,

You are always a book.

Sometimes read,

Sometimes put down.

Whether you care or not,

You are always a mountain.

Sometimes climbed,

Sometimes enjoyed from afar.

Whether you know or not,

You are always a road.

Whether I walk on you or not

You are still there.

Then you and I

Are not far from each other, and not close to each

other either.

Then you and I

We sit, we are quiet.

爱

我的爱

不是

无影无踪

我的心

不是

无声无息

我的情

不是

无心无肺

我的爱

不是

无情无义

Love

My love,

Is not

Without a trace.

My heart

Is not

Quiet in silence.

My mood

Is not

Heartless.

My love,

Is not

Ruthless.

云说

我观云

云自在

我阅水

水好深

云说

你在天上

我就在地上

你在岸上

我就在水底

我在地上

望天

云淡风轻

我沿岸漫步

浅底祥云

云说

我有山

我有水

云说

我不在天上

也不在地上

云说

你行我静

你走我行

不过山

不越水

云说

有也一时

没有也一地

祥云是一朝

流云也只一夕

The Cloud Says

I look at the cloud

The cloud is free.

I read the water

The water is deep.

The cloud says

You are in heaven

I'm on the ground

You are on the shore

I'm under water.

I'm on the floor,

To Look up at heaven

The Clouds are pale and the breeze is light.

I walk along the shore,

Auspicious clouds are overhead.

The cloud says,

I have mountains,

I have water.

The cloud says,

I'm not in the sky,

I'm not on the ground.

The cloud says,

When you walk, I will be quiet

When you go, I will go.

I don't go over mountains

I don't fly over the water.

The cloud says,

When you own something, it will last only a moment

When you lose something, it will be in a moment.

Auspicious clouds stay just in an instant

Drifting clouds appear in a flash, too.

心在

今天

我是那自在的王

我的心

宽容与自由

处处可见

言论自由

真实

即刻

在在处处

心

藏着无数的

珍宝

无数的喜悦

美乐

顷刻间

广大无边

妙不可言

心在

悟道

还是悟到

空

是虚空

无限的虚空

静

是寂静

无限的寂静

我是自由的王

来来去去

上上下下

哭哭笑笑

疯疯癫癫

我是妄想的王

神仙之王

我摸

心在

虚空里

我是那么渺小

如尘埃

如发丝

心在

空了

我就不在了

我在

心却不在了

虚空尽是虚空

静还是静

愿无边

空到寂静

With My Heart

Today

I am the king of freedom.

My heart,

Is tolerant and free

Everywhere we see

Speech is free.

Truth

Is immediately

Around us.

In the heart

Hides innumerable

Treasure

Countless joy

And gladness.

In an instant are

Vast brimless and

Too Wonderful.

With your heart

Attain enlightenment

Or just realize

Emptiness

Is empty

Infinitely empty.

Silence

Is quiet

Unlimitedly quiet.

I am the king of freedom,

I come and go

Up and down

I cry and laugh

I am crazy and mad.

I am the king of delusion,

King of gods

I touch

My heart is

In the emptiness

I am so small

As dust

As a piece of hair.

The heart is here

If it becomes empty

I will be gone,

If I'm here

The heart is gone.

The emptiness is empty

The silence is quiet.

May the Ananta

Be boundlessly empty.

下一站，你在哪里

究竟人生去向哪里

这一辈子

为了富贵

还是爱情

从来没有去过天堂

真的不知道

如何想象

它在什么地方

常见到路边的银行

和华丽的宫殿

听说

天上会掉钱

可我从没见过

有人说

有钱能使鬼推磨

可多少人

因无钱气短

常听讲牛郎织女

也听过嫦娥奔月

见过

两情相悦

没见过忠贞不渝

相逢一笑

恍若隔世

下一站你在哪里

你知道

我不知道

The Next Stop, Whither You Go?

Whither do we go?

Should the whole life

Starve for wealth and honor

Or for love?

Have never been in heaven,

I really don't know

How to imagine.

Where is it?

I often see banks by the road,

And fabulous palaces.

It is said that,

Money will drop from heaven.

But I've never seen it.

Some people say,

Money makes the mare go

But there are so many people

Suffering from lack of money.

I heard of the cowherd and the weaving maid,

The Goddess Chang'e flying to the moon.

I've seen

Resonance between two lovers.

But I've never seen an unswerving love.

We meet with a smile

A lifetime seems to have passed.

Where is your next stop?

You know the answer,

But I don't.

我爱这世界

我爱

这黑不是黑

白又不是白

苦又不苦

甜又不是甜

不知何味的世界

我怀疑它

又有什么办法

它是那么

丰富精彩

又是那么无限博大

那么不可思议

这个世界

我恨过

可又有什么办法

天还是天

地还是地

恨只是一个

短暂的错误

我爱这个世界

我走过的路

看过的风景

穿过的峡谷

呼吸的空气

还有我心中

阅读过的脸色

我爱这个世界

一个人如在虚空

面对生活的快乐

也想狂喜地逃亡

那里是天堂

那里是故乡

我爱这个世界

因为它白不是白

黑不是黑

因为它不可捉摸

无常的虚空

让我的爱

无法和你招呼

我不知道

三界内有多少虚空

人和人有多少无常

时空变换

有多少因果

在因缘聚合时

瓜熟蒂落

从这座灵山

到那座灵山

一步步不知道

究竟要走多远

这个世界

黑究竟还是黑

白还是白

这一天

我有些明白

光明的灯盏

只能照见一片世界

太阳也只是照见

一半白天

这个世界

就是黑不是黑

白又不是白

我爱这个世界

不黑不白

不明不暗

不苦不甜

不生不熟

从地球上任何地方

开始

都会一样

这是个事实

I Love this World

I love

This world, where black is not black,

White is not white,

Bitter is not bitter,

Sweet is not sweet,

The intangible world.

I doubt it,

But what can I do?

It is so

Rich and wonderful.

It is so infinite and vast.

It is so incredible.

This world,

I hate it.

But what can I do?

Heaven is still heaven,

Land is still land.

To hate is just one

instant mistake.

I love this world.

The road I've walked on,

The scenery I've seen,

The canyon I've passed,

The air I've breathed,

And those faces in my heart,

Which I have read.

I love this world,

Alone in the emptiness,

I face the joy of life,

Sometimes even want to flee in ecstasy.

Where there is heaven,

There is home town.

I love this world,

Because it's not white

or black.

Because it's unpredictable.

The emptiness,

Stops me from greeting you

With my love.

I don't know

How much emptiness is there in the three realms?

How much impermanence do people suffer?

By the transformation of time and space,

How many karmas

At the harmonized time,

Shall come to the end.

From this soul mountain

To that soul mountain,

Step by step, without knowing

How far should we go?

In this world

Black is black

White is white

This day

I understand something

The light of brightness,

Can only beacon a corner of the world.

The sun can only light

A half of the day

In this world

Black is not black

White is not white

I love this world,

Neither black nor white,

Neither bright nor dark,

Neither bitter nor sweet,

Neither strange nor familiar.

From anywhere on earth

You start

It will be still the same,

Which, is a fact.

爱是无量光

Love is Amitqbha

谁的手

谁的手

抚慰我的心灵

没有一丝安静

谁的心

让我放弃追求

躺在失眠的床上

谁的爱

让她化在风中消失

没留下任何尘埃

谁的手

她让我靠近

无穷无尽的无奈

对视

那一天

照顾好你的灵魂

Whose Hand

Whose hand

is soothing my soul

that has no peace.

Whose heart

Stops me from desiring

Lying sleeplessly in bed.

Whose love

Makes her disappear in the wind

Leaving no trace, not even a dust.

Whose hand

Makes her draw me close

Endless helplessness.

Look at

The day,

Take care of your soul.

远逝的阳光

远逝的阳光

和一把锁

是一双眼睛

留下的

痕迹

远逝的阳光

和一把锁

我的一生

都像是

深藏不露

The Dying Sun

The dying sun

With a lock,

Is what a pair of eyes

Left behind.

The dying sun

With a lock,

My whole life

Looks like

A diamond in the rough.

有一世

有一世

手持华盖

莲花

上品

有一人

手捧莲花

笑口

常开

有一声

心存净土

福慧

无边

有一爱

清静无为

真空

妙有

有一生

遁入空门

寂灭

超生

有一天

因缘聚合

花开

自来

There Is a Life

There is a life,

When you hold a canopy

And a lotus,

The most beautiful one.

There is a person,

Holding a lotus,

Grinning

All the time.

There is a voice,

With a pure heart,

Murmuring for brimless

Happiness and wisdom.

There is a love,

Quiet, inactive,

A wonderful existence

In real emptiness.

There is a lifetime,

You become a monk,

Experiencing a Nirvana

And a reincarnation.

There is one day,

Destiny brings us together,

When the flowers are in bloom,

All will come by themselves.

歇即菩提：家在东南常作西南别

弘一法师说

悲欣交集

时间只是时间

没有春夏秋冬的节气

人终究是人

逃不过生老病死

人终究是人

躲不过恩怨情仇

又是一个年轮

为了庆祝用灿烂的烟花爆竹宣告辉煌

倒不如为了解开究竟的束缚痛哭一场

过年就是过年

歇即菩提

那

就是一瞥

亦是涅槃

是心

Let Go, and You'll be Rewarded with the Bodhi: I Live in the Southeast, but I Often Leave for the Southwest.

Master Hong Yi said,

Grief and joy come simultaneously,

Time is just time.

There are in fact no such solar terms as the four

seasons,

After all, man is just a man

Who can't escape from life and death.

After all, man is just a man

Who can't ignore love and hatred.

One more annual ring is coming out,

You can celebrate the festival with brilliant fireworks,

Or you can have a good cry to get rid of inquisitions.

A new year is just a new year.

Let go, and you will be rewarded with the Bodhi,

That

Is a glimpse,

Is the Nirvana,

Is the heart.

把我的心注在静谧的空中

把我的心注在静谧的空中

我不想在大地上

拥有太多的内容

我在繁华的世界

学会了虚荣

如果我能像一棵树那样站着

我一定会招致风的赞扬

我不想以一棵草的形象出现

因为我

不想左右摇摆

我的心拥有丰富的内容

我想注在静谧的空中

不致让谁开采

Keep My Heart in the Quiet Air

Keep my heart in the quiet air,

I don't want to be on the earth

With too much affairs to worry about.

Me, in the bustling world,

Learn to be vain.

If I could stand like a tree,

I will surely get the wind's praise.

I don't want to appear as a grass

Because I

Don't want to swing to the left and right.

My heart is full

I want to stay in the quiet air,

Where no one can exploit me.

在行走中闭关

我的爱

在水面上漂行

西下的夕阳

艳舞的飞天

在宁静的世界

忏悔

感恩

喜悦

祝福

寂静的天神

让我深抚大地

静静流泪

我在流水中看到

夕阳

还有夕阳的影子

美

从灵魂中

流淌了出来

一滴一滴

落如甘露

洗一身沧桑

这个黄昏的相遇

让河流无声

船舶停行

人生没有苦等

几世的回眸

换今生通体的光芒

洗一世风尘

我求天求地

翻山越岭

那一刻

如此相见

我心怀感恩

隔世的经忏

终于

见一地莲花

无边的吉祥云彩

那一刻

风也有情

云也有情

我深怀感激

泪流满面

在行走中闭关

终于相见

Retreating While Walking

My love

Is drifting on the water.

The setting sun in the west

Is like an apsara flying, dancing.

In a quiet world, I

Confess,

Thank,

Enjoy,

And pray for happiness.

Silent gods

Let me caress the earth.

Quietly I weep.

In the running water I see

The sunset

And its shadow.

The beauty

Flows out

From the soul,

Drop by drop,

Falling like dew

I wash away the aged weariness.

Our encountering at this dusk,

Lulls the river,

Stops the ship.

We don't wait in vain.

Looking for you in the past several lifetimes,

Finally, our bodies are covered with glory in this life.

Washing away the old fatigue,

I pray to heaven and earth,

I tramp over hills and dales.

At that moment,

I meet you finally.

I am grateful

For several lifetimes'confession,

At last

Make me see the lotus,

And boundless auspicious clouds.

At that moment,

The wind is affectionate,

The cloud is sentient.

I am so grateful

And burst into tears.

Retreating while walking,

We finally meet.

在河边

夕阳西下

暮色花影

走到河边静观花语

人一静下来

坐在河边就觉得有些空了

河谷上空时有飞鸟缓慢而行

河面上时有鱼儿轻划水面

这一切都让你沉浸下来

静静地坐下来

风自然就吹到了脸上

微微地有点凉

虫子的声音也悄然来临

我静静地体会这个时空的安宁

在这片宁静的时刻体验空

空是一个什么样的东西

这个念头一闪而过

一个人坐在河边

在宁静的世界里

我爱上了水中月影

风中的虫鸣

香河中的鱼伴

还有对面的灯光

墨黑的树影

当虫子开始合唱

风渐渐大了

河面的鱼儿也次第舞蹈

我看到波光粼粼的水面闪动着无数细碎的幸福

这些东西一时间随顺心念

无声无息地散开

一个单独的心灵究竟有多富足

只有真正体验过才会知道

有人问

一个人坐在河边

发生了什么事

这个世界上还有什么能与寂静同在

寂静之美胜于无声的世界

唯有爱

才能够清明地活在当下

By the River

There is the setting-down sun,

And the flower's shadow in the twilight.

I walk to the river quietly to watch the flowers.

When I calm down

Sitting by the river, I feel a little empty.

There are birds flying slowly over the valley,

There are fish paddling in the river,

These all make you immerse into meditation.

I sit still,

The wind touches my face.

It's a little cool.

The insects' voices come quietly.

I enjoy the peace of this moment and this space.

I taste emptiness in this quiet moment.

What is emptiness?

The question flashes by.

Sitting by the river alone

In a quiet world,

I fall in love with the moonlight in the water,

And the insects' singing in the wind,

The fish's company in the fragrant river,

The lights on the other side,

And the dark shadows of the tree.

When the insects begin to chorus,

The wind is getting stronger.

The fish in the river dance one after another.

I see the glimmering water sparkling with countless

pieces of happiness.

All these, merging in my heart,

Scatter again without a sound.

How consummated can a lonely soul be?

I know the answer, only when I have experienced it.

Someone asks

A man sitting by the river alone

What's happening?

What else in the world can be compared with silence?

The beauty of silence goes beyond the silent world

itself.

Only love

Makes you live in a pure way in this moment.

生

死

只为一夕而存

就此了断

千万不舍

万般无奈

一生皆为还债

谁说心无挂碍

谁说从头再来

真死

即是痛快

Live

Death

Lasts only a second,

You break away from everything

However you grudge

However you hesitate

You have paid your debts, you die.

Who says there will be no worries?

Who says you will start all over again?

True death

Is a real joy.

那个……那个

那个　风

不待你开口

就来了

那个　雨

不等你撑伞

就晴了

那个　人

不声不响

就走了

那个　你

不知不觉

就不见了

That... That

That wind

Doesn't wait for you to speak

It just comes.

That rain

Doesn't wait for you to find shelter

It just stops.

That man

Making no reply

Just leaves.

You

Without being noticed

Just disappear.

布达拉宫的城墙

那云

不升不降

那树

不高不矮

随着人流

走在拉萨的街头

不紧不慢

在布达拉宫的城头

心无所住

那才是幸福的王

将心静在那儿

不上不下

不喜不悲

在八廓街上转塔的人啊

在那个不变的旋转中

心花怒放

在法喜的汪洋中

即使那突然飘落的雨

和那雨后出现的彩虹

都是洗尘接风的仪轨

在心中化成

一滴滴甘露

玛吉阿米的酥油茶

让人静静地体悟

那份法乳的清凉

蓝天白云

雪域的高原

是心灵的圣地

在大昭寺的街头

从此不离不弃

静谧无语的心空

不言不语

阳光普照

万物生长

心灵的大门通往天堂

一步一拜

我的心

不再丈量远方

而是

让无量的光芒

穿过布达拉宫的城墙

照耀着四方

The Walls of the Potala Palace

The cloud is

Neither rising nor falling.

The tree is

Neither tall nor short.

With the stream of people

I walk along the streets of Lhasa

Neither fast nor slowly.

On the top of the Potala Palace

I find nowhere to dwell my soul.

There is the king of happiness.

Who dwells his soul here,

Neither up nor down,

Neither happily nor sadly.

Those who turn around the pagoda on the Barkhor

Street,

Form an eternal circle,

And sink in ecstasy.

In the ocean of Dharma joy

Even a sudden rain

And a rainbow after that

Are simply a part of the ritual of reception.

In our mind they all change into

Drops of nectar.

Makye Ame's buttered tea

Quietly brings a man into

Dhamma's blitheness.

The blue sky and white clouds

The snowy plateau,

Are the holy land for the soul.

On the streets of Jokhang Temple

We will never be apart from each other.

The quiet and speechless heart

Utters not a single word.

The sun shines,

And all things grow.

The gate in our heart will lead us to heaven

One kowtow, one step,

My heart

No longer measures the distance

But

Feels boundless light

Go through the walls of the Potala Palace

Illuminating everywhere.

一杯水的静逸

敬一杯水

就是供养佛

佛

真正的供养

是放下后

皈依

佛

皈依

法

皈依

僧

有时候

一杯水的静逸

是动态的

潇洒的

无上的自由

安静的飘逸

很宽广的气质

很优美的风度

一个人

在一杯水的世界里

能悟到什么？

The Serenity of a Cup of Water

To toast a cup of water

Is to worship the Buddha.

For the Buddha

The real worshipping,

Is to let everything go,

To convert to the Buddha,

To convert to the Dharma,

To convert to the Buddhist.

Sometimes

The serenity of a cup of water

Is dynamic

And unrestrained.

Supreme freedom,

Quiet elegance,

Broad temperament,

And graceful demeanor,

In a cup of water.

What can you see?

爱是通向天堂的路

爱是自由的灵魂

坐以观心

清净无挂碍

爱可以传递

尽虚空遍法界

喜欢不是爱

喜欢只是一种清爽

一个单纯的世界

是容易被感动的

在无语的世界

有更多的单独与寂静

真的能除一切苦

爱是慈悲和感恩升华的智慧

当你去爱这个世界

一花一草一沙一石

就拥有了丰富的觉性

于是有人说

闭门即是深山

可想在这个世界

爱是多么地丰富

即使一刻的参悟

也会灵光闪现

人啊人

谁能无情呢

这一念即是深山

多清净啊

当你在这个当下一默如雷

静谧而安详地独坐

当你拥有一个美好的世界

爱即是妙吉祥

那人说得好

观自在菩萨

行

感恩这个世界

如此爱你

Love is the Way to Heaven

Love is the soul of freedom,

If you sit in introspection,

You will feel quiet and unhindered.

Love can be passed on

All through the emptiness and the dharma dhatu.

To like is not to love

To like is a refreshing feeling.

A simple world

Is easy to be moved.

In a silent world

There will be more solitude and silence,

Which can really drive away all sufferings.

Love is the wisdom sublimated by compassion and gratitude,

When you love the world,

Its flowers, grass, sand and stones

Will be endowed with rich awareness.

So someone says

Closing the door, you will be like practicing in a mountain.

It can be imagined that in this world

How rich love is

Even a moment's enlightenment

Shines with glory.

Oh, man

Who can be merciless?

A single thought brings you to the deep mountain.

How peaceful that will be!

When you're silent in this moment,

Sit alone in peace and quietness.

When you have a wonderful world,

Love is Manjushrimitra.

The man says well

The Bodhisattva Avalokita

Is walking.

Please show gratitude to this world

For loving you so much.

自由

窗外的黄昏

有一只飞翔的鸟

她将纤细身影横穿

天空

土地

河流

森林

在她飞旋的

瞬间

留下一个白色的弧

她的一切包含着奥义

这是一本打开的书

所有的文字都浅显明白

然而

她的语义在

遥远的风中

像一棵粗大的

菩提

在生命的拔节中释放

禅义

我的自由烙刻着

痛苦的文字

在浩瀚的人海里

欲望如流

自由被扭曲

在规范之中

高度悲伤的

灵魂承认

一切虚妄的幸福

都宛如昙花

物质的欲望

是受伤的

精神的渴求

是伤人的

在生命的长廊上

自由

是一个独行的神

她在心灵明亮的时候

放松

爱或恨都在一天中流浪

昨天将不再因她的好恶回头

在一个无风的晚上

点上一种光荣的梦想

让她在天堂中熠熠发光

我已爱过世界所有的一切

唯有你将陪伴我的生命

在岁月的散步中

进行语言的游戏

外面的景色是属于我们的

只是我已不再要求

完美

在心灵没有极限的度数中

用你的美丽测量她的温度

我不会在最烫的时候

说因为自由的情感而退出

这沿传千年的法则

Freedom

In the dusk outside the window,

A bird is flying.

Her slender figure traversed

The sky

The land

The river

The forest.

In her flight

Suddenly

She leaves a white arc.

All her actions are meaningful.

This is an open book

With plain words

However

Her meaning

In the distant wind

Is like a big

Bodhi tree.

Spreading in the growing life

The idea of Zen.

My freedom is stamped with

Painful words

In the vast sea of faces,

Desire flows.

Freedom is distorted

In the norm

The extremely sad soul

Recognizes that

All fake happiness

Is just like the short-lived Epiphyllum flower.

Material desires

Are desires of

The wounded spirit

Which hurts.

On the corridor of life

Freedom

Is a solitary god.

When her heart is bright

She relaxes.

Love or hatred wanders in the day.

I said yesterday that I would not look back because

of her opinions.

On a windless night,

Light a glorious dream,

Let her shine in heaven.

I've loved everything in the world,

Only you are with me in this life.

In the walk of time

We play the game of language.

The view outside belongs to us

While I don't ask anymore

For the perfection.

With the infinite degrees of the mind

Please use your beauty to measure her temperature.

I won't quit when the temperature is the highest,

For the freedom of emotions

Such is a rule that has a thousand years' history.

寒山寺访僧——雨中见花猫

我闻花鸟声，

声声有余痕。

寒山下小雨，

初心已湿润。

钟亭门外人，

问我干什么。

花猫从前过，

也想翻经书。

Visiting Monk of Hanshan Temple—
Drizzle Showed a Tabby Cat

Birds were heard, flowers were smelt

More sounds than marks were left

Light rain fell on the cold mountain,

Initial heart went wet.

The man outside the Bell Pavilion,

Asking me where to go, what to do.

A tabby cat passed by,

Willing to read the scripture as well.

在行走中闭关

Being in silent retreat while walking

禅思的玄机

文／叶橹

　　国人向来对自身的生存方式有所考量，并因之而总结出许多处世之道。积极参与社会生活者谓之"入世"，淡出江湖者为"出世"；得道升天的人会标榜"达则兼济天下"，失意落魄之后就会"穷则独善其身"。诸如此类的人生哲理，其实都离不开对个人命运的关注。非常奇怪的是，人生哲理尽管五花八门，儒释道混杂交融，我们民族却常常自认为是一个没有宗教信仰的民族。依我之见，自古迄今我们所总结出的许多处世之道，大抵都是一种"权变"的产物。

　　没有终极的价值观，虽然也有"不以成败论英雄"的说法，但那大多是一种自我安慰的托辞；在社会的普遍意识中，还是把"成王败寇"奉为圭臬的。细细想来，国人的智慧虽然不输于任何国家和民族，可是所受的灾难和痛苦，也同样不输于别人。也许正是因为如此，近些年来信佛入教的人日渐增多，可能是想从精神上找到寄托吧。

写下以上这些文字，是读了校尔康诗集《在路上》而生出的联想。我虽然读过一些禅诗，还写过论洛夫的禅诗的文字，但对佛学却几无所知。读校尔康的诗，深感他已经是一个佛家的修行者，诗中处处流露出一种禅诗的睿智，我还能对他的诗说些什么呢？

首先引起我好奇的是，校尔康本是理工科大学生，为什么会走上参禅悟道的佛门之途呢？他的诗在某种程度上回答了这个问题。他对生活的爱和恨，他对万物和诸多生命现象的观察和思考，使他走上了禅思之路。我由此就想到，以往我们常把归入佛门的叫作"出世"，说他们是"看破红尘"之人，因而做了"出家人"。现在想想，这种说法似乎流于浅薄。《般若波罗蜜多心经》有言："色不异空，空不异色，色即是空，空即是色。"这里对色与空的相互依存和合二而一的存在关系，说得十分透彻而辩证。所以用"出世"来形容佛门子弟，并不恰切。因为他们对诸多万物和生命现象的思考，仍然在我们生活的世界之内。

不过话还得说回来，佛门子弟们尽管并未"离世"，但他们的禅思方式还是异于许多世俗观念的。这也正是它能够吸引众多人走上参禅悟道之路的根本原因。一般人似乎认为，进入佛门的人，大抵都是在现实生活中受了重大的精神打击而看破红尘者。不可否认有这样的皈依者。但是真正有佛心者，其实是因大爱而生的。校尔康有一首《我爱这世界》，写的就是他内心深处的感受：

我爱
这黑不是黑
白又不是白
苦又不苦
甜又不是甜
不知何味的世界

这不白不黑不苦不甜而不知何味的世界，正是它的"色"。而"它不可捉摸"的"无常的虚空"，正是它的另一种存在。校尔康实实在在爱慕的，甚至有时候也是恨着的，正是这"地球上任何地方"都一样的"事实"。面对这样一个"事实"，校尔康才有可能以阔达的心胸、灵动的思维，展开他的翅膀翱翔于天地之间。

作一篇小文，我不可能在这里对校尔康的诗作出详尽的评析，但是我想指出一点——他的诗性思维的灵动性。他的灵动性一方面表现为对一些抽象事物和观念的诗性陈述；另一方面则是在具象化的事物中获取到抽象的升华。不妨信手拈来《远逝的阳光》为例：

远逝的阳光

和一把锁

是一双眼睛

留下的

痕迹

远逝的阳光

和一把锁

我的一生

都像是

深藏不露

这短短的两节诗，把阳光和锁的意象，置于不同的场景中而蕴涵着各自不同的意味。前一节是外貌的过程性陈述，而后一节则是内观心灵的探究。或许这样的诗不能给你一个明确的答案，但它的答案其实已经在文字的陈述中。至于如何理解它，则有赖于各人的生活体验和悟性了。

校尔康说他自己是一个带发修行的人，其实剃不剃发只是一个形式而已。以我这个俗人之见，参禅悟道是一个人对现实社会和自身生命存在的审视。从终极意义上说，任何一个人都是向死而生的，参悟生死之大道，是一个有自觉的生命意识的人毕生的修行。

从校尔康的许多诗中，我们已经读出了他对生命的所着重与彻悟，在他的视域内，许多无意识的生命成为有意识的生命，或者说，这些本来是有意识的生命，被人们误认为无意识的了，而校尔康以自己的慧眼识破并揭示出它们的真相。能做到这一点，不正是他生命价值的体现吗？

不妨以他的一首诗回赠予他：照顾好你的灵魂！还加一句：写出更好的诗！

The Subtlety of Zen Thoughts

By Ye Lu

The Chinese always like to think about their way of life, and sum up a lot of life philosophy. Those who actively participate in social life are believed to have the so-called "worldliness"; while those who fade out of the secular world show a kind of "aloofness". Those lucky ones will advertise a life philosophy of "being successful and benefiting the world", and those who are frustrated say that we should "be poor and alone". Such philosophies of life, in fact, are inseparable from the concern for personal destiny. It's very strange that, although we have various philosophies of life and mixed thoughts of Confucianism, Buddhism and Taoism, our nation often thinks itself as a nation without a religious belief. I think many of the philosophies we have summed up since ancient times are the products of "compromising".

We have no sense of an ultimate value. We do say that "A hero is not necessarily a final winner", but most of such beliefs are results of self-consolation. We still, in fact, take it as a norm that "winner takes all" generally. If you think about it carefully, you will realize that although the wisdom of Chinese people is not inferior to that of any other countries or nations, the disasters and pains we have suffered are no less than those of others, either. Perhaps that is the reason why more and more people believe in Buddhism in recent years: to find spiritual solace.

The above are what came to my mind, reading the collection of poems *On the Road* by Xiao Erkang. Although I have read some Zen poems and once commented about some written by Luofu, I have little knowledge of Buddhism. When I read Xiao's poems, I felt that he has already been a

Buddhist practitioner. There is wisdom of Zen in his poems. I'd like to say something about that if allowed.

First, what intrigues me is why Xiao Erkang, originally a major in science and engineering, should embark on the path of Buddhism. To some extent, his poetry answers this question. His love and hate in life, his observation and thinking of the world and our life made him turn to Zen thinking. It occurred to me that we used to call those who convert to Buddhism as being "aloofness". We say that they are the people who are "out of the world", that they become "ascetic". Now, it seems to be a superficial statement. "Prajnaparamita Hrdaya" has a saying:

"Form is emptiness and emptiness is form. Form is no other than emptiness, emptiness is no other than form." The interdependence of form and emptiness and their mutual existence are very clearly and dialectically stated here. Therefore, it is not appropriate to use "aloofness" to describe Buddhists. Their observations on things and life are still located within this world.

However, it should be said that although Buddhists do not go "out of the secular", their way of Zen thinking is still different from many secular ideas. This is the basic reason why many people are attracted to embark on the road of Zen and Buddhism. Common people seem to think that the ones who believe in Buddhism are mostly those who are disillusioned by great spiritual blows in real life. There is no denying that part of the converts are in such a situation. But the ones who have a true Buddhist heart are born with great love. There is a poem "I love the world" written by Xiao Erkang, which states such beliefs lying in his deep mind.

I love

This world, where black is not black,

White is not white,

Bitter is not bitter,

Sweet is not sweet,

The intangible world.

This world is not white, not black, not bitter, not sweet and everything is intangible. This is the complicated part of the world. Meanwhile, the "unpredictable and impermanent void" works as the simple part of this world. If you put the two parts together, you see the full world. It is this true world, which you can see "anywhere on the earth", that Xiao Erkang really loves and even hates sometimes. By facing such a "true world", Xiao Erkang spreads his wings to soar between heaven and earth with a broad mind and a flexible thinking.

It is impossible for me to make a detailed comment on the poems of Xiao Erkang in such a short essay. But still, I would like to draw your attention to the fact that his poetic thinking is flexible. His flexibility, on the one hand, is expressed as the poetic description of abstract things and ideas; on the other hand, turns out to be a sublimation of concrete images into abstract thinking. Here, I will take "The dying Sun" as an example.

The dying sun

With a lock,

Is what a pair of eyes

Left behind.

The dying sun

With a lock,

My whole life

Looks like

A diamond in the rough.

These two short stanzas put the images of sunshine and a lock in different scenes, producing different meanings. The first stanza is a progressive statement of the appearance, and the second stanza is an exploration of the inner mind. Such a poem doesn't seem to give you a clear answer to life, but the answer is already in the verse. How to understand it depends on everyone's life experience and savvy.

Xiao Erkang said that he is a Buddhist practitioner

without shaving his hair away. In fact, shaving or not is just a form. If you ask me, Zen meditation is a person's review of the society and his own existence. In the ultimate sense, anyone is born to death. To understand life and death is a lifelong task of any person with an independent consciousness.

From many of Xiao's poems, we can see what he emphasizes and understands in life. In his vision, many unconscious lives have become conscious ones, or in other words, they are originally conscious lives mistaken for unconscious ones. And Xiao Erkang, with his insight, sees through and reveals the truth. Is such an achievement not the embodiment of his life value?

Please allow me to urge him with one of his own lines: Take Care of Your Soul! If one more line: Write Even Better Poems!

禅趣与义理的诗意呈现

文／王巨川

　　校尔康诗友，之前并不熟知，但这本诗集，我还是很认真地读了一遍。可以看出，这本诗集是诗人对自己存在的世界的另一种解释，其中蕴涵着的禅趣与义理通过诗歌的形式呈现出来。并且在许多诗歌中，诗人有意无意地把中国传统的禅宗意境与禅悟思维承传下来，在彻悟中还原万千事物的"本来面目"。

　　禅诗是中国传统诗歌流脉中非常重要的一支，诸如陶渊明、李白、苏东坡、王维、黄庭坚等大诗人都有诗作留世。现代诗人李金发、废名、穆旦与卞之琳等人的诗歌中也都可以捕捉到中国传统禅宗美学的心机与情结，台湾诗人洛夫也是禅诗的写作高手，被誉为"'现代禅诗'的写作者"。而校尔康的诗歌，也可以纳入"现代禅诗"的写作范畴，其诗歌既有中国传统禅诗的精神气韵又不失现代诗歌的表现技巧，把自己对禅（禅宗）的理解贯注于诗歌的表现之中。

校尔康的诗歌写作最大的特征就是禅趣与义理的结合，这就为其诗歌本身赋予了深刻的内涵和境界，并且能够在日常的禅悟中呈现诗意之美。我们普遍认为"禅宗美学的核心问题是境界—意境"，王国维也有"意与境偕"之说，认为"境界之呈于吾心而见于外物者，皆须臾之物。惟诗人能以此须臾之物，镌诸不朽之文字，使读者自得之"。因此我们看到，校尔康将这本诗集命名为"在路上"，本身就是一个禅宗开悟的偈语，不仅仅是设定了一个诗集的名称，同时也为他的诗歌写作营造出一个境界，就像诗中最后说的"在路上 / 我们只观此生 / 悟到了如来 / 却到不了彼岸"一样，是对人类从来时到去时的整体观照，这种对生命过程的彻悟使得他能清晰地理解人生的意义。其中《下一站，你在哪里》《即使，于是》《谁的手》等诗歌中也同样在诗意的字里行间追问终极的禅趣与义理，诗集中大多数的诗歌都是诗人自我体验后生发出来的禅悟。

校尔康通过禅悟把日常性体验通过诗歌来呈现，并且融入诗人的理性判断，这是他诗歌的一个显著特征。禅诗需要一种空境、一种智慧，而这种空境、智慧的获取更在于禅诗语言喻指的某种禅境、智慧。应该说，校尔康的诗歌语言是干净而纯粹的，比如"敬一杯水 / 就是供养佛"（《一杯水的静逸》）、"我的头发

长满树枝 / 在心灵上蔓延 / 在出售鲜花的年代"(《我》)。这些貌似不经意的语言随着诗意的流动形成了一种禅境，抑或说是一种诗性的艺术智慧。

短短的一篇小文无法全面概述校尔康的诗歌成就和艺术特色，但不管怎样，这本集子中所呈现的每一首诗歌，都能参悟到他在诗中所凝注的"禅"和"诗"的深刻之意。他力图把传统禅诗与现代气息结合起来，从而达到一种新的精神指向，我想这也是这本诗集的最大的特点。

The Poetic Presentation of Zen Thoughts and the Common Sense

By Wang Juchuan

I am not quite familiar with Xiao Erkang, but I have read his collection of poems very carefully. This collection is another interpretation of the poet's own world, in which the implied Zen thoughts and the common sense are presented in the form of poetry. In many of these poems, the poet intentionally or unintentionally inherits the Chinese traditional of Zen conception and Zen awakening, and restores the "original faces" of the world as a result of thorough comprehension.

Zen poetry is a very important branch of Chinese

literary tradition. For example, Tao Yuanming, Li Bai, Su Dongpo, Wang Wei, Huang Tingjian and other great poets all wrote Zen poems. In modern poetry written by such poets as Li Jinfa, Fei Ming, Mu Dan and Bian Zhilin, we can also capture the ideas and emotions unique to Chinese traditional Zen aesthetics. The Taiwanese poet Luo Fu is also a master of Zen poetry and is known as a "Modern Zen Poetry Writer". The poems of Xiao Erkang can be included in the category of "modern Zen poetry", too. They show both the spirits of traditional Chinese Zen poetry and the skills of modern Zen poets, conveying his understanding of Zen in those delicate lines.

The most characteristic feature of Xiao's poetry writing is the combination of Zen thoughts and the common sense, which endows his poetry with profound connotations and a wide realm and helps him to capture poetic beauty in daily Zen meditations. We generally believe that "the core issue of Zen aesthetics is the concept of ideal-Realm". Wang Guowei also has a theory of Ideal-Realm. He said,

"The Realm is a reflection of the Idea in my mind. The Idea is conveyed as the Realm by means of instant images. Only poets can use such instant images to produce eternal lines, which allow readers to understand the Realm that is suggested by the poets." Therefore, we can see that Xiao's title of this collection, i.e., *On the Road*, is a conveyer of Zen awakenings itself. It not only sets the name of the collection but also creates a realm for his poetry writing. Just as the last words in his collection, "On the road/We only see this life/Enlightened of the Buddha/While reaching no Faramita", *On the road* is an overall observation of life process whence we come and whither we go. This understanding of life process allows him to clearly see the meaning of life. Among his poems, such as "The Next Stop, Whither You Go" "Even, Then" "Whose Hand" and others also pursue the ultimate Zen conclusion and the common sense with poetic words. Most of the poems in the collection record the poet's own Zen enlightenment from his life experience.

It is a remarkable feature of Xiao Erkang's poetry

that he often combines enlightenment in daily life with his rational judgement. Zen poetry needs a realm of emptiness and wisdom, while the conveying of such a realm depends on the use of Zen metaphors. Such emptiness and wisdom lie in the metaphor of the language of Zen poetry. It should be said that Xiao's language of his poems is clean and pure, as goes in such lines as "To toast a cup of water/Is to worship the Buddha" (*The Serenity of a Cup of Water*), "Branches are mingled in my hair/Spread in my heart/In the flower-selling era" ("I"). These seemingly easy language form a kind of Zen realm, or poetic artistic wisdom, with the flow of poetic feelings.

This short article can't fully summarize Xiao's poetic achievements and artistic features. But still, I should say that every poem in this collection is blessed with the profound relation between Zen and poetry, which is what he has been endeavoring to fuse into his works. He tries to combine traditional Zen poetry with a modern flavor to achieve a new spiritual direction. I think it's also the greatest characteristics of this collection.

佛禅诗人校尔康
——路上的禅思者

文／庄小明

校尔康的诗集给人一种印象——一位孤独的僧人，扛着手杖，迈着坚定的步子，走在行人寥寥的路上。他的行李很小，普通人实在无法理解他如何在路上度过漫长的岁月。但他其实还负着另一个东西，诗意，光晕一般随行，使得他的生活、生命，获得了另一种存在方式。

校尔康踏入佛禅之路，颇有传奇色彩。他出生于江苏姜堰，祖籍内蒙古，祖先为蒙古黄金家族乞颜部孛儿只斤氏，据考证系成吉思汗的后代。他曾在南京理工大学读书，后混迹于珠江路的碌碌红尘谋生。2009 年在南京九华山依传真法师学禅修道，并在玄奘寺带发修行，四年后从师命下山访道参学。

在一般人的理解中，信佛追禅，意味着一种对人生的澄净、超越，而校尔康从他的修炼之途中，最终开悟到：爱，才是信仰的真谛。他的诗篇《爱是通向天堂的路》，可谓他对这种"爱"的一种阐述、命名，并赋予其现代的光辉。诗篇一开始，诗人便咏出"爱是自由的灵魂"，由于信仰的力量，这种爱超越了世俗的羁绊，穿越了物欲的魔障，"尽虚空遍法界"，展开灵魂的翅翼，自由地飞翔。这种爱，"能除一切苦"，使孤独寂静发光，使一花一草一沙一石，"拥有了丰富的觉性"。实际上，在某种意义上，诗集《在路上》中的诗篇，就是来自这种对万事万物的爱的光线的折射。

佛禅的中心问题"空""虚"，与老子的"道"一般，一直挑战着后人的思维与想象能力，具有无穷无尽的可阐发的诗性空间，校尔康作为一位佛禅诗人，对此自然会有属于自己的体悟。他有一首诗《问禅：花之心》，通过一位禅者与一位侍者的对话，展开了对一朵花的"空"的探索。在现实的感知中，花之心应在花瓣花蕊的簇拥中，然而，当一切都摇落净尽，只剩下空枝的时候，侍者继续问禅者："花有心吗？"禅者说："有！"一旁的诗人，由此听着欢喜，因为他得到了一种启悟、共鸣：一朵花的"空"，就在一朵花的心，在花瓣花蕊的簇拥中。经过一个摇落的历程后，这空枝上的"空"，已不仅是一朵花的"空"，而成了一种生命的"空"、一个世界的"空"，或者说，成了某种宇宙的中心。"空"的意义，由一朵微小的花，而获得了无穷的弥散，获得了无限的诗意空间。

这种"空"的意义，在《大吉祥云：烟花散时虚空无尽》中，有着清晰的呈现："炸裂过后烟花散尽//突然发现进入了一个虚空/在所有因缘和合的时候/那是一个中心/世界的中心"。在《心生便是罪生时》中，更有着美妙的延伸："真空是/人们与心灵间/纯洁的连接"，这里，"空"不仅是一种中心，还成了一种水晶桥梁，引渡着人们纯真的心灵。无疑，诗集《在路上》的这类诗篇，是佛禅诗人校尔康具有代表性的作品，既有着古典禅诗的顿悟，亦有着现代新诗的理的展开，相融无间，浑然新篇。在表现形式上，这些诗篇亦不拘一格，有纯诗体，有寓言体，有对话体等，且语言舒卷自如，自由清新，契合着作者追求的禅境。这些都为中国当代禅诗的创作注入了值得关注、珍惜的新品质。

从某种意义上讲，每个人都走在自己的路上。有些人浑浑噩噩地尾随着前面的人群，却总是发现走错了路或走过了站，处于不断的懊恼中；有些人匆匆忙忙奔向某个向往的终点，满怀希望却发现什么也没有，而坠入绝望。显然，这些都与校尔康的世界无涉，作为一位在路上的行者诗人，他关注着每一个与他相遇的事物，以自己的禅性在这些事物上开启一扇扇门，而进入一个诗意葱茏的世界，丰富完善着自己的人生。然而，一个人如何才能拥有自己的禅性呢？诗人在《门：在路上》一诗中，引用了《金刚经》中的一段名言："一切有为法，如梦幻泡影，如露亦如电，应作如是观。"通俗一些说，就是要把生命看透彻了，把世界看"空"了，"觉醒／才会／自然而然地发生"，人与所遇事物之间的那扇门，也就自然开启了。

与一个事物相遇，即有一扇门，而与事物的不断相遇，便出现一扇又一扇的门——正是这一扇扇的门，构成了行走之"道"，这是校尔康的《门与道》这首颇为玄秘的诗告诉我们的。在这首诗中，诗人并没有以得道的高人自许，或像某些常见的"高僧"那般故意玩弄玄虚，他像一个真诚的友人一般，袒露着他行走在这条"道"上时的探索、困惑：

但常常
是无路可走

处处
似十字路口

并非所有的门，都可以轻易打开，因为诗人并不能完全割除他的肉身，肉身仍会在某个时刻显示出它的欲望、重量，成为一种魔障。即使进入一扇门后，诗人又会面临一个新的选择，如在十字路口，因为一扇门并不会告诉他下一扇门的方位或"道"的方位，一切还得靠自己继续探索下去。但诗人以这样的体悟鼓励着我们，以及他自己：

从未体验过
就不会
自然生长

实际上，也正因为此，我们才得到了佛禅诗人校尔康。一条透彻的大道，恐怕只能得到一些偈子，而不会得到真正的诗歌。校尔康本质上是一个以佛禅探索世界的诗人，而他的探索，亦使佛禅具有了更浓郁的诗意。诗集《在路上》中的一些最有特色和感染力的诗篇，就可谓诗人开启一扇扇门时的复杂心理呈示。《无相》一诗，写诗人一次遇到一群飞鸟，他撒下一碗米，期待鸟们能来与自己对话，一同愉悦于"雨后落花：带我穿过山门"的禅意。但现实的状况是，诗人虽向往"生公说法顽石点头"，但他清楚自己并没有真正通鸟语，亦不知道鸟的"觉性"能否感知自己的心愿。在这扇诗人与鸟之间的门前，诗人陷入了"子非鱼，安知鱼之乐"的悖论，徒然诉说着自己的期待，而鸟始终一言不发。诗的最后，诗人抓了一把落花抛起，"风一吹有些飘进水里／有的落到脚边"，似乎暗示我们，答案就在这落花、流水、风中。

在另一首诗《解脱》中，诗人由听到一只鸟的"破空而鸣"，突然联想到"落花流水／生命无常""照见五蕴皆空"。在佛禅的要义中，世界的本质就是一种空，一种大寂，"不生不灭／不垢不净／不增不减"，然而，在这由鸟声偶然启开的一扇门前，诗人却犹豫起来，"人世间的沧桑与世间人的悲伤突然升起"。在这里，校尔康的诗人身份与他的佛禅信徒的身份发生了冲突，他并不想永久居住于"五蕴皆空""无限的寂静"，他只是想借此来到达"花开花落／来去自如"之境——他想转向另一扇门。但冲突似乎并未解决，作为一个佛禅信徒，他不时地感到世界的空无、寂灭，而他作为诗人追求的"花开花落／来去自如"之境，在这个冷酷的现实世界，实际上倒是很难抵达。最终，他干脆痛快地让自己"放开大哭／泪奔如流"，以一种颇为世俗的方式，完成了一次解脱。

一场痛哭，并不能解决信仰问题，但在不断的探索中，校尔康寻觅到了自己本真的生命，并以此定位了自己的信仰。我与校尔康尚无面缘，但依我从他的诗中得到的粗浅理解，他定位的信仰，应是一种佛禅与老庄融合后的禅宗。《留得残荷听雨声》

一诗中，讲述了诗人与一位得道者的相遇。得道者告诫诗人：世事崎岖，如履薄冰，唯有远遁没有人迹的地方，方能见到世界的奇观。诗人则回应了自己的追求：花开花落，顺其自然，无论是穿越崎岖世事，还是踏入人迹罕见处，都只是生命的一个过程。这首诗中，诗人心境萧远，然而拥有了一种宁静。

拥有了心境的宁静，并不意味诗人在路上的脚步将变得平缓，而是变得更为平稳、坚定。校尔康天性是一位行者、思者，他思考时间，思考终极，思考痛苦，思考死亡，思考再生，思考他所触及的一切，于是，有了这本《在路上》。但所有的一切，都不可能有终极答案，校尔康只是以他的禅思，为我们这个僵化的物质世界打开一扇扇诗意的窗户，让我们领略到人生的另一番风景。只要他还在发现着，就会在这条寂寞的路上继续走下去，因为他是如此地爱着这个世界，爱着"你"：

在路上
我不辞辛苦
转山转水
只想遇到你

在路上

我顶礼焚香

一心一意

就想求到你

在路上

我戒情戒义

时时刻刻

皈依你

在路上

我从从容容

无知无觉

就路过了你

……

——《在路上》

A Buddhist Zen Poet Xiao Erkang— a Zen Meditator on the Road

By Zhuang Xiaoming

The poetry collection of Xiao Erkang gives an impression that a lonely monk, carrying a cane, is taking firm steps on a lonely road. His luggage is so little that common people can't understand how he survives on such a long road. But in fact, he has shouldered another thing, poetry, which like a halo accompanies him and offers him another way of existence.

The way that Xiao Erkang converts to Buddhism is quite legendary. He was born in Jiangyan, Jiangsu Province. His ancestral home is Inner Mongolia and his ancestry belonged to the golden family of Borjigin, offspring of Genghis Khan. Xiao once studied at Nanjing University of Science and Technology, and later made a living in the bustling world of Zhujiang Road. In 2009, he studied Buddhism in Jiuhua Mountain in Nanjing, learning from Master Chuanzhen, and practiced in Xuanzang Temple. Four years later, he followed the master's order to do a Buddhism visit, so he went downhill.

In common people's understanding, the belief in Buddhism and pursuing Zen means a kind of clarity and transcendence over life. On the way of his cultivation, Xiao Erkang finally realizes that love is the essence of faith. His poem "Love Is the Way to Heaven" can be described as an elaboration or naming of this "love", which also endows such a love with some modern glory. At the beginning of the poem, the poet chants "Love is the soul of freedom". Because of the power of faith, this kind of love transcends the fetters of the secular world, goes through the barrier of material desire, "Discovering the Emptiness of the World".

Such love spreads out the wings of the soul, and flies freely. This kind of love "Can drive away all sufferings", making loneliness and silence shine; endowing the flowers, grass, sand and stones "with rich awareness". In fact, in a certain sense, the poems in the collection *On the Road* all shine with such boundless glory.

The central themes of Buddhism are "emptiness" and "void", which, just like Lao Tzu's "Tao", always challenge the thinking and imagination of future generations and offer an inexhaustible poetic space to be elucidated. As a Buddhist and Zen poet, Xiao Erkang has his own understanding of them. His poem "Ask Zen: Heart of Flowers" describes a dialogue between a Zen master and an attendant. Xiao explores the "emptiness" of a flower. In the perception of reality, the heart of a flower should be surrounded by petals and stamens. However, when everything else is shaken out, only the empty branch is left. The attendant continues to ask the master: "Does the flower have a heart?" The master says, "Yes!" The poet listens to them joyfully, because he is enlightened at the moment that the "emptiness" of the flower lies just in its heart, even surrounded by petals and stamens. After a shaking-out process, the "emptiness" on the empty branch has become not only the "emptiness" of a flower, but also the "emptiness" of life, or even the world. In other words, it becomes the center of a certain universe. The meaning of "emptiness" is thus achieved from a tiny flower for infinite dispersion in an infinite poetic space.

Such meaning of "emptiness" is clearly expressed in "Auspicious Clouds: Endless Void after the Fireworks", "After the explosion, the fireworks were scattered/I suddenly found myself in a void/The time of all karma being harmonious/That is a core/A center of the world." In "Sin Occurs When Feelings Occur", there is a wonderful extension: "The emptiness is/what is between people and the soul/It's a pure connection". Here, "emptiness" is not only a center, but also a crystal bridge, connecting people's pure mind. There is no doubt that this kind of poems in the collection *On the Road* are the representative works of the Buddhist Zen poet Xiao Erkang, which has both the epiphany of classical Zen poetry and the rationalism of modern poetry. It blends both into one and becomes a new type. As to the form of expression, these poems are not limited to one style. There are traditional poetry, allegories and dialogues, etc. The language is comfortable, free and fresh, which is in line with the author's pursuit of Zen. All of these have brought important and precious new elements into Chinese contemporary Zen poetry.

In a sense, everyone is on his own road. Some people blindly follow the crowd in front of them, always finding that they have gone the wrong way or missed the station, and thus constantly sinking into frustration; some people rush to a desired destination, but find nothing they expected, and fall into despair. Obviously, all these have nothing to do with the world of Xiao Erkang. As a walking poet on the road, he pays attention to everything he meets, opens a door for them with his Zen nature, and enters a poetic world that enriches and refines his life. However, how can one have his own Zen nature? In the poem "The Door: on the Road", the poet quotes a famous saying in *the Diamond Sutra*: "All conditioned phenomena are like a dream, an illusion, a bubble and a shadow, like dew and lightning. Thus, please look at the world in this way." Generally speaking, we need to thoroughly understand life and see the world as an "emptiness", then "Awakening/Will/Naturally happen". The door between people and the things we meet will open by itself.

When you meet one thing, there will be a door, and when you meet things constantly, there will be doors one after another. Such doors show us the "way" of walking, as told in the mysterious poem *Doors and Ways* by Xiao Erkang. In this poem, the poet doesn't boast to be an enlightened man, or kick up a cloud of dust like some common "eminent monks". He is like a sincere friend, revealing his exploration when walking on the "road". He is confused:

But often

There is no way

Everywhere

Is like a crossroads

—Door and Way

Not all doors can be opened easily, because the poet cannot completely break away from demonic barriers which will still show its desire and weight. Even after entering a door, the poet will have to make a new choice, just like at the crossroads, because the door will not tell him the location of the next door or the "road", and all has to be explored by himself. But the poet encourages us, and himself, with such understanding:

Never experiencing

One would never

Naturally grow

—Door and Way

In fact, it's because of such difficulties that we now have the Buddhist Zen Poet Xiao Erkang. With an easier road, I'm afraid we can only get some verses, but no real poems. Xiao Erkang is essentially a poet who explores the world with Buddhism, and his exploration makes Buddhism more poetic. Some of the most characteristic and influential poems in the collection *On the Road* can be described as the complex psychological revealing of the poet when he opens the doors. In the poem "No Form", the poet once met a group of birds. He sprinkled a bowl of rice, expecting the birds to come to talk with him and enjoy the Zen scene that "Fallen flowers after the rain: take me through the monastery gate". But in reality, although the poet yearns for such a realm as "A word from the wise is sufficient", he knows that he does not really understand the birds, nor does he know whether the "awareness" of birds can perceive his wishes. In front of the door between the poet and the birds, the poet falls into the paradox of "You are not the fish; how do you know what constitutes the enjoyment of fish?" He has told his expectation in vain, while the birds never say a word. At the end of the poem, the poet grabs some fallen flowers and throws them up.

"Some were blown into the water, some fell to my feet." It seems that the answer lies in the fallen flowers, in the water and the wind.

In another poem "Moksa", the poet suddenly hears the "roaring" of a bird, which reminds him that "Flowers fall and water flows/Life is such a capricious one" and "Light shedding on the five skandhas and finding them equally empty". In the essence of Buddhism, the substance of the world is a kind of emptiness, or great silence, "Neither produced nor destroyed; neither defiled nor immaculate; neither increasing nor decreasing." However, in front of the door accidentally opened by the sound of birds, the poet hesitates, feeling that "the vicissitudes and the sadness of the world come to my heart suddenly". Here, the identity of Xiao Erkang as a poet conflicts with his identity of a Buddhist and a Zen believer. He doesn't want to live permanently in the "emptiness of five skandhas" or "infinite silence". He just wants to get to the realm where "flowers bloom and flowers fade, all things just go naturally." —He wants to turn to another door. But the conflict doesn't seem to be solved. As a Buddhist and Zen believer, he feels the emptiness and oblivion of the world from time to time, and it's very difficult for him to reach the realm from this cold and realistic world, the realm where "flowers bloom and flowers fade, all things just go naturally". In the end, he "Just let go and cry/ pour out the tears" in a rather secular way and gets some relief.

Tears cannot solve the problem of faith, but in the continuous exploration, Xiao Erkang has found his real life and has positioned his faith. I haven't met Xiao Erkang in person, but according to the rough understanding I get from his poems, his positioned belief should be a kind of Zen which is integrated into Buddhism and Taoism. In the poem "The sound of the Rain with Withered Lotus", the poet talks about his meeting with an enlightened person. The latter one admonishes the poet: the world is rugged, and living here is like walking on the ice. Only when you are far away from people, can you see the wonders of the world. The poet responds with his own pursuit: no matter how flowers bloom and fade, just let it be. Whether it needs to go to the rugged world, or walk into rare places, they are just a process of life. In this poem, the poet's mood is depressed, but he has peace.

Having peace of mind does not mean that the poet's steps on the road will be smooth. Rather, they become more stable and firmer. Xiao Erkang is a walker and a mediator in nature. He thinks about time, the ultimate, the pain, the death, the rebirth and everything he touches. So, he has this collection of poems *On the Road*. But nothing has an ultimate answer. Xiao Erkang just opens poetic windows for our rigid material world with his Zen thoughts and lets us appreciate another landscape of life. As long as he is still exploring, he will continue to walk on this lonely road, because he loves the world and "you" so much:

On the road

Take all the trouble

I walk around mountains and lakes

Hoping to encounter you.

On the road

I worship and burn incense

With heart and soul

Eager to pray for you.

On the Road

I cut off my love and emotions

At every moment

Always trying to convert to you.

On the road

I take my time

Without noticing

I pass by you.

...

On the Road

哦，是这一个家伙

文 / 李青崧

听说您是江湖高手，我慕名而来，请问您能不能指点我一二？

高手看看我，微笑着说：您吃饱了没有……

会飞的鸟还是要回来……

这是我有缘在读到校尔康行者诗集《在路上》的两篇意味深长的结尾，其中之禅机犹如书法之飞白、国画之留空，让我沉思，引我会心。

这一部分，或许令您云里雾里，莫名其妙……

对！就是这个妙，妙不可言，无理而妙！好像刚过门的新媳妇，无理取闹！可就是这一闹啊，把小两口的感情推向高潮一样，此时诗中的无理而妙把心推向了高潮……

这，诗中之禅，弦外之音，好比禅门公案中参话头之起疑情一样，让你大疑大悟，顿生桶底脱落杯碎念空、照破山河尘尽光生和云在青天水在瓶之自在之境……

正如《门：在路上》：

心
安在路上
觉醒
才会
自然而生地发生

又如《门与道》：

重重之门
都是道
但常常
是无路可走

再看《在行走中闭关》：

这个黄昏的相遇

让河流无声

……

在行走中闭关

终于相见

印心而来，化空而去。

于《在路上》次第排开，成为一道独特的风景！

会心处，真如醍醐灌顶，豁然开朗……

这是一个现代诗人，更是一个"在行走中闭关"、在红尘中修心炼性的现代行者，在以禅入诗、以诗悟禅并以诗示禅之殊胜诗禅法门修持中和身心豁然中，犹如蚕儿满腹经纶时不吐不快，亦如禅师用功成熟之时桶底脱落水花四溅一样，尔康师兄在"闭关"中"开悟"时呈现出了有别于常人独具意蕴的禅意境界……

所谓悟境即空境，禅意即无意。恰恰用心无，无心恰恰成。可谓道法自然，妙契天真，说不清道不明，但深有怦然心动的感觉，这就是禅味。正如山果野葡萄的滋味，你的舌头被全部化掉了还说不出是什么味道；亦如一阵香风扑来，你的鼻子被全部漫掉了还说不出是什么风。漫城过客的禅意陡然涌出啊，你的心顿被彻底空掉了还道不出是什么，只知骤然身心照亮，全体呈现，一片空明，无上清凉……

正如尔康兄常常在诗中戛然而止一样，惭愧我也不知全象只能点到为止！相信高明的读者自当会兴会无前，无须我在此饶舌，而早日水落石出真相大白：

哦，原来是这个家伙……

丁酉九月初一凌晨初成于京华弘乐源

九月初五凌晨续于智峰大灵

Oh, This Guy

By Li Qingsong

"I heard that you are a great master. I take the trouble to find you. Can you give me some advice?"

The master looked at me and said with a smile, "Have you had your lunch?"

"Flying birds are still coming back..."

These are the two meaningful endings that I have read about in Xiao Erkang's collection of poems *On the Road*. Such Buddhist allegorical words are like the half-dry brush of the Chinese calligraphy and the blank part in a

Chinese painting, which makes me meditate and lead me to awakening.

Maybe you are confused by what I said.

But yes! That's where subtleness lies. Being so, so wonderfully meaningful, that words fail to express them. A newly-wed wife sometimes makes trouble for no reasons in her new home. But it is this trouble that pushes the love of the young couple to the climax. Similarly, the irrational subtleness in these poems push readers' emotions to the climax.

The overtones in these poems are just like the mysterious plots in the Zen Cases. They make you suspicious, awaken you in a sudden, and bring you into a totally free and clear space.

As is said in "The Door: on the Road":
A heart

Peacefully on the road

Awakening

Will

Naturally happen.

Another example is "Doors and Ways":

Doors over doors,

Are the ways,

But often

There is no way

Then, look at "Retreating while walking" :

Our encountering at this dusk

Lulls the river

...

Retreating while walking

We finally meet

From the heart, for the empty.

These poems are lined up in the collection *On the Road*, becoming a unique landscape!

The enlightening words suddenly make you feel refreshed and click into place...

Xiao Erkang is not only a modern poet, but also a modern practitioner who "meditates and walks in seclusion" and cultivates his mind in the world of mortals. In the practice of being a Zen poet, and being enlightened by writing poems and at last teaching Zen with poems, Xiao Erkang is just like a silkworm who has to get the wisdom off his chest. He is also like the legendary Zen master. When he is consummating at his work, the bottom of his barrel falls off and water splashes down. He shows the unique realm of Zen achieved by him during his seclusion.

The so-called enlightenment is in fact emptiness, and Zen is unintentional. To go naturally is the key idea. To follow the nature, to keep innocent, to remain unspeakable, but still profoundly touched, that is Zen. It's like the taste of wild grapes, which your tongue, even if soaked in the fruit's juice, will not tell its taste. It's also like a sweet wind, which your nose, even if is completely covered by it, will not tell its smell. The Zen enlightenments that Xiao Erkang pour out will make you feel that your mind has been completely emptied and still you can tell nothing. You just know that suddenly your body and mind are lit up, and everything is clear, empty and blithe.

Just as Xiao Erkang often stops abruptly in his poems, I think I'd better not give a full view of the poet, so I will only say the above words about him. But I believe that wise readers will be inspired by Xiao's poems, and I don't need to be too talkative here. The truth will come out by itself.

Oh, here comes the guy...